The Marshal of Babylon

The Marshal of Babylon

A Shawn Starbuck Western

Ray Hogan

THORNDIKE
CHIVERS

This Large Print edition is published by Thorndike Press®, Waterville, Maine USA and by BBC Audiobooks, Ltd, Bath, England.

Published in 2004 in the U.S. by arrangement with Golden West Literary Agency.

Published in 2004 in the U.K. by arrangement with Golden West Literary Agency.

U.S. Hardcover 0-7862-6887-5 (Western)
U.K. Hardcover 1-4056-3129-5 (Chivers Large Print)
U.K. Softcover 1-4056-3130-9 (Camden Large Print)

The text of this Large Print edition is unabridged.
Other aspects of the book may vary from the original edition.

Set in 16 pt. Plantin by Elena Picard.

Printed in the United States on permanent paper.

British Library Cataloguing-in-Publication Data available

Library of Congress Cataloging-in-Publication Data

Hogan, Ray, 1908–
    The marshal of Babylon : a Shawn Starbuck western /
Ray Hogan.
        p. cm.
    ISBN 0-7862-6887-5 (lg. print : hc : alk. paper)
    1. Starbuck, Shawn (Fictitious character) — Fiction.
2. United States marshals — Fiction. 3. Missing persons —
Fiction. 4. Brothers — Fiction. 5. Large type books.
I. Title.
PS3558.O3473M38 2004
    813′.54—dc22   2004055306

The Marshal
of Babylon

1

Shawn Starbuck, halting in a pool of deep shadows, allowed his gaze to run the dusty, weathered façades of the structures standing shoulder to shoulder along Dodge City's Front Street.

He had just ridden in, had stabled his horse, and was now beginning a tour of the town's many saloons in search of one Jim Winfield, a man he hoped might give him information as to the whereabouts of his missing brother, Ben — known also as Damon Friend.

Winfield was only a slim lead, one picked up back in southwest Texas where the man had been employed as a cowhand on Price Hagerman's Hash Knife ranch. It was thought that Ben Starbuck also worked there, but no one presently riding for the outfit could be sure. Only Winfield could be positive, and he had moved on to Dodge when Shawn, doggedly following a cold trail, arrived.

Starbuck had ultimately ridden on, having discovered long ago that any clue to Ben, however small, must be tracked down as traces of his brother were few. Thus, locating Winfield and having a talk with him was more important.

He would go first to the Long Branch. The bartenders there were said to know everyone, to be virtual directories of all those who came to, and spent any amount of time in, the brawling cow and buffalo town at the end of the railroad.

Hitching at the pistol slung low on his left thigh, Shawn moved away from the wall of the building near which he had paused and struck off down the boardwalk. There were few persons abroad at that early evening hour since it was just supper time and the night's activities were yet to begin. It was Shawn's hope to make as many inquiries concerning Winfield — and Ben — as possible before the saloon men became too busy to engage in conversation.

Starbuck's steps slowed — halted. A tall, lean individual dressed in dark trousers and broad-brimmed hat and wearing a star on the pocket of his white shirt had emerged from one of the structures immediately ahead and was moving slowly away.

Almost immediately three dark figures stepped in behind him from the adjoining building. Light glinted dully on the blade of a knife held poised to strike by one.

Shawn reacted quickly. He stepped off the walk, gained the center of the street in a half a dozen strides, stopped.

"Marshal!" he called into the closing darkness. "Behind you!"

The lawman threw himself to one side, wheeled. Starbuck's hand swept down to the forty-five on his hip, hung there as the lawman's arm lashed out. Using one of the long-barreled pistols he carried as a club, he smashed it into the head of the man with the knife and dropped him to his knees.

As the two others jerked back, spun, and started to run, he brought them to a hasty stop.

"One more step and you're dead!"

Shawn, hand still riding the butt of his own weapon, eyes on the pair frozen in their tracks, crossed to the sidewalk. The lawman did not turn to him, simply continued to stare at the two men. They were unarmed, Shawn noted, as was the one on his hands and knees now shaking his head groggily.

"Get him on his feet," the lawman snapped, kicking the knife off into the dark-

9

ness at the base of the building. "We're taking a little walk to the calaboose."

Only then did he turn to Starbuck. "You the one doing the singing out?"

Shawn nodded, feeling the man's eyes take swift inventory of him and pause as they reached his holstered gun.

"There's a law against wearing a weapon north of the tracks. You know that?"

Starbuck shook his head. "No, I didn't."

The badge on the lawman's shirt said Deputy Marshal. He studied Shawn for a long moment. "Just ride in?"

"About an hour ago."

"First time in Dodge?"

"First time."

"Reckon that explains it,'" the deputy said. "Help me herd these jaspers to jail, and I'll tell you what's what around here . . . Name's Earp. Yours?"

"Starbuck," Shawn replied, and stepped up to the lawman's side.

Earp bobbed his head, reached out with an open palm, and gave the nearest of the three men a shove toward the corner. As they all moved off, he turned to Shawn, a dark, hard-faced man with a flowing, handlebar mustache.

"Obliged to you. I'd've dropped all three of them if you hadn't hollered."

Starbuck nodded. "Or they'd have got you."

Earp considered Shawn again in that cool, level way of his. "Yeh, maybe there was a chance of that, too. Anyway, it's a favor I owe you, and I'm paying a part of it now. Any lawman in Dodge could shoot you for wearing a gun on this side of the deadline. It's the law. But I'm overlooking it, seeing as how you didn't know."

One of the outlaws laughed. Earp, tone hardening, said, "Maybe you'd like buffaloin', same as your friend there got."

The man wagged his head hurriedly. "No, sir, Mister Earp — no, sir! I was only thinking the law seems to apply to us Texans, but it don't to nobody else."

"It goes for every man riding into Dodge no matter where he's from."

"Well, I ain't so sure —"

"That's coming close to calling me a liar!"

"No — no, sir! Just saying how it seems," the man said hurriedly, stumbling a little in the dark.

"It does, no matter what you think," the deputy said. He glanced at Shawn and shrugged. "Texans all feel like the law here in Dodge has it in for them. Not the truth. It's just that they give us more trouble than anybody else."

"Maybe that's because there's more of them. Lot of herds coming up from Texas."

"Expect that's the reason, all right, but that don't give them the right to take over the town — which is what they're always trying to do. So far they ain't had much luck, but they're sure working at it. A bunch of them's got together and offered a thousand-dollar bonus for any man who'll lay me out for Boot Hill. Reckon that's what these jaspers were after — that bonus . . . Calaboose is right over there. . . ."

An elderly man with a shotgun cradled in his arms met them at the doorway of the jail. He put his weapon aside and took charge of the prisoners.

"What's the charge, Wyatt?" he asked as he clanged the cell door shut and turned the key.

"Disturbing the peace," the deputy answered in an offhand way, and swung to Shawn. "Expect you'd best leave that iron of yours here."

Starbuck reached for the ornate silver buckle with the superimposed ivory figure of a boxer on its polished surface, tripped the tongue, and handed the belt, holster, and weapon to the lawman.

Earp studied the buckle curiously. "You

some kind of a champion fighter?"

Shawn's shoulders moved slightly. "Belonged to my Pa. He was a boxer — got his training from some Englishman."

"And you?"

"Taught me, too, same as he did my brother, Ben. That's the reason I'm here, Marshal. Looking for him. Could be going by the name of Damon Friend."

"Ben Starbuck . . . Damon Friend," Earp murmured, continuing to examine the buckle. "Name ain't familiar. What's he look like?"

"Haven't seen him in ten years or better. Chances are we look pretty much alike. Could be I'm some taller."

The deputy shrugged, then glanced at the jailer. The older man shook his head.

Earp said, "I guess if he ever showed up around here, we missed him. You sure he did?"

"I'm not sure of anything — not even that he's alive. I've been chasing back and forth across the country for quite a spell trying to find him."

Earp handed Starbuck's gear to the jailer, who hung the belt on a peg on the wall. Sauntering to the doorway, the deputy halted and threw his glance down the street, now bright with lamplight.

"What made you think he'd be here in Dodge?"

Shawn settled on the edge of the desk. "Wasn't the reason I'm here. It was a fellow he worked with, I think, down in Texas, that I came to see. I wanted to ask him if he could tell me anything about Ben — where he went after he left Hagerman."

"Hagerman?"

"A rancher down in southwest Texas."

"I see. Who was this bird? Could be we'll know him."

"Winfield. Jim Winfield."

Earp wheeled slowly, touched the jailer with his flat, dark eyes, came back to Shawn.

"Reckon we can tell you about him, all right."

Starbuck pulled himself upright. The long ride to Dodge City had not been for nothing after all. "Good. I'd like to know where I can find him."

A remoteness came over the deputy. He folded his arms across his chest, leaned forward slightly.

"He a friend of yours?"

"Nope, never met him. I was just told he might know Ben. He in town now?"

"Sure is. Permanently. We planted him up on Boot Hill."

14

2

"Boot Hill!" Starbuck echoed. "You mean he —"

"Buried him there a couple months ago. Leastwise, was a man of that name. Skinny bird, dark hair, scar on the left side of his face."

"I wouldn't know about that," Shawn said in a falling voice. "Like I said, I never met him, only knew him by name. What happened?"

"Got hisself shot to death," the jailer said. "It was right down in front of Zimmerman's lumber yard."

"Seems he had words with Tom Agar one night in Dog Kelley's place. Agar's a gambler," Earp added. "Then next morning he jumped Agar. He had a pistol hid inside his shirt. Only thing, Tom was toting a gun, too. Derringer. Put two forty-one-caliber slugs in your friend before he could get off a shot."

Starbuck stirred wearily. "I guess that finishes that," he murmured.

The jailer moved in behind the desk and sank into the chair. "Why'd you say you was looking for him?"

"He's hunting his brother, Frank," Earp explained. "This Winfield knew him. Starbuck figured he maybe could tell him where he is."

The older man bridged his fingers, nodding slowly. "I see . . . Well, was I looking for somebody, I'd do it the easy way. I'd take me over to Babylon and just set there and wait. Whoever I was hunting'd be sure to drop by some day."

Shawn shifted his attention to Frank. "Babylon? What's that?"

The old jailer stared, dug into his pocket for a plug of tobacco. "You sure are new around here if you ain't never heard of Babylon — or the Babylon Palace!"

"Only place with that name I know of was one in the Bible."

Earp laughed. "This one probably ain't much different. It's a town about a day's ride to the south."

"Biggest, fanciest place you'll ever set your peepers on," Frank said, biting a corner off the plug. "All kinds of gambling — things a man ain't never heard of. Then there's drinking and dancing — and the women. Man and boy, they're real lookers! Everyone there'll bug out a fellow's eyes like he was a tromped-on lizard!"

Starbuck's shoulders moved again. "Still never heard of it."

"It ain't been there too long. Couple of years, maybe," the deputy said. "The whole works belongs to a couple of jaspers that blew in from the East, I heard. Built what they call the Babylon Palace, added some stores and houses for the help to live in, and named the town Babylon. Sure is quite a layout, all right. Mighty fancy. Somebody said they spent ten thousand dollars alone on just furnishing the place."

"Which they get back every month," Frank said. "Punchers, pilgrims, drifters — they just plain flock to it. Seems a man ain't lived 'til he seen all them pretty women McGraw and Fisher've brung in or had his pockets cleaned out at the Palace's tables."

"Women are all young, too. It's sort of the specialty of the house," Earp said. "They keep fifteen or twenty on hand all the time just to draw business. McGraw brings them in from all over the country. He's got an eye for the prettiest, they say, and once he spots one, she ends up sooner or later in the Palace."

"It's Fisher that looks after the gambling end of it," Frank continued. "He's mighty sharp, but folks all claim he's honest. Never did hear no complaining from fellows who'd bucked him.

"And there's a plenty of them. Expect just about every man this side of the Platte has been to Babylon and tried his luck at the tables and had his time with one of the girls — excepting you . . . Now, was I hunting a man, that's sure the place I'd go to look."

Starbuck glanced at Earp. The lawman nodded. "Frank's right. Chance of you finding this brother of yours in this part of the country will be better there than anywhere else I can think of."

The jailer shifted his cud. "And if he ain't there now, he's been there or he'll be coming by soon, can bet on that," he declared confidently.

Earp signified his agreement. "I'd go there, and if you don't spot him first off, ask around. One of the girls or maybe one of the dealers will recollect him. If they don't, just hang around, wait. He'll show up."

"I was just thinking about the hitchrack in front of the place," Frank murmured.

18

"Longest one I ever drawed a horse up to. Must be two hundred foot from one end to the other. Man could picket a whole army at it!"

Shawn listened in silence. Babylon did sound as if it had good possibilities. "You say it's a town?"

"More or less — anyway, I reckon you'd call it a town. But McGraw and Fisher own the whole shebang. They've got a hotel and a restaurant along with a stable and a few other stores. Have their own law — a town marshal, jail and all. And McGraw's the judge. He got himself appointed, all legal, somehow. They keep things pretty straight, too, even if they do get some of the wild bunch right along.

"There was a big jasper wearing the badge when I was there once," the jailer rambled on. "Meaner'n hell, he was. I seen him crack open two or three skulls right there in the Palace. Name was O'Neill, as I remember. One thing he sure done was keep order."

"Left there and went to Wichita and got himself killed," Earp said. "Somebody said a fellow he'd roughed up bad in the Palace was the one who done it."

The lawman paused, cocked his head to one side as a staccato of gunshots echoed

19

faintly in the night. The sound came from the area beyond the railroad tracks.

"Seems things are warming up down there," the deputy murmured absently. Then, "Figure to try your luck in Babylon?"

Shawn shrugged. "Sounds like a good bet — and I've got no other leads to follow. Winfield was my only hope here."

"I'm laying odds you'll stumble across something there," Frank said. Rising, he reached for Starbuck's gun, paused. "Aiming to pull out tonight?"

"No. Been in the saddle all day. I think I'll get myself a room in a hotel, leave in the morning."

The jailer settled back. Earp made a motion with his hand. "Give it to him anyway," he said. Then turning to Shawn, he added, "Don't wear it. Keep it rolled up under your arm, and when you get to your room, leave it there — unless you're planning to spend some time tonight below the deadline."

Starbuck smiled. "I think I'll pass that up. Right now all I'm wanting is a good meal and a soft bed."

Earp nodded. "Glad to hear it. Strangers don't do too good down there unless they know how to take care of themselves."

Shawn turned toward the door. "Doubt if it's any worse than Whiskey Row or Juarez City or a couple other places I've found myself in," he said dryly. "Reckon I'd make out."

Earp looked Starbuck up and down appraisingly, nodded. "Yeh, expect you would. You got some place special in mind to stay the night?"

"No, I have to find —"

"Come on with me then," the deputy said, stepping out into the street. "I'll take you to a friend of mine. He'll put you up."

3

It had been an all-day ride across an endless pasture of buffalo grass that had been varied only here and there by needle-sharp yucca plants, scattered clumps of sage, and an occasional tree. A persistent wind, hot for that late in summer, had fanned his face, parching his throat, and he had looked forward to reaching Babylon with its reputedly fabulous Palace.

Now, finally, with the vast prairie behind him, no longer resounding to the thunder of buffalos' hoofs but marked only by their bleaching bones, and the journey over, Shawn halted in the center of a wide clearing and stared at the edifice rising before him.

The Palace was all that Deputy Marshal Earp and his jailer friend had said it would be — and more. Lifting its two-storied bulk off the flat upon which it had been erected, it squared itself against the clean

Kansas sky in a flamboyant flourish of Gothic windows, scrolled cornices, mirrored insets, carved corbels, and Corinthian columns, all accented with red, gold, and glaring white paint.

A broad porch ran its full width, but there were no chairs available — an unspoken invitation for all to enter and do their loafing inside, it would appear. As Frank had noted, the hitchrack matched, perhaps even exceeded the building's reach, offering station for numberless horses. The three dozen or so dozing hipshot before it now required but a fraction of its capacity.

At the right and connected to the imposing structure with plain, unpretentious countenance was a livery stable, a feed store, and last in line, the marshal's office and jail. Beyond those Starbuck could see a wagon yard, a low-roofed, rambling affair resembling an ordinary ranch bunkhouse, and still farther yet, where a stream cut a narrow path across the flat, a scatter of small huts all looking exactly alike in a bleak, neglected way.

Off the opposite end of the Palace came first a hotel that, like all other business concerns, was nameless. It devoted one corner area to a restaurant. Adjoining it was a barber shop offering, besides expert tonsorial attention, a hot tub-bath and painless dentistry. At the end of the connected row was a saddle-and-gun store that also carried a stock of trail grub and other supplies.

Starbuck's gaze absorbed it all while he marveled at the thought of two men alone giving birth to such a phenomenon in so incongruous a place; and viewing such splendor recalled to his mind the great cathedrals and kingly mansions depicted in the books Clare Starbuck would read from to him and Ben during the long winter evenings on the Muskingum farm.

The accomplishments of man had awed him then just as did this mingling of many distinct and separate architectural styles, and while such would be an abomination to the purist, Starbuck nevertheless recognized in its conglomerate grandeur a victory over the desolate sameness that typified the false-fronted buildings of the frontier.

Brushing his hat to the back of his head, Shawn grinned. Babylon — the place was aptly named and likely no less wicked than its biblical counterpart. At the crossways of trails running north to south, east to west, it undoubtedly drew men of all kinds —

and among them would be Ben.

He sobered, his square-cut face darkening, his gray-blue eyes filling with a remoteness as he thought of his brother. Although a man still young in years, the mark of experience lay upon him, and as he sat his sorrel horse with an unconscious ease, the presence of cool capability shrouded him like a cloak of caution.

He was tall, his six-foot height evident even while yet mounted, and there was a leanness to him, but it was a trail-acquired, muscular leanness rather than a thinness. The suppleness of his muscles as he spurred the gelding into the hitchrack and swung down bespoke the perfect coordination of his being.

Again he glanced about. He would get something to cut the dryness in his throat, then check in at the hotel, he decided. Later, when the night's activities were in full swing, he would visit the Palace and make his inquiries. Securing the sorrel, he stepped up onto the porch, crossed to the embellished double doorway, aware now of the hubbub of sound within the building, and entered.

Starbuck halted abruptly. The interior of the Babylon Palace was as awe-inspiring as the exterior. It appeared to be one huge room, the colorful ceiling of which was supported by countless, garishly decorated columns. Dozens of chandeliers laden with glowing lamps dispelled any darkness and shadow while multiplying their number in the solid bank of mirrors behind a mahogany bar extending almost the entire width of one wall.

Well to his right he could see a small stage affair near which were two pianos, a drum, and several musical instruments. Close by was a door painted bright red and upon which was lettered the word *Office*. Similar entrances adjoining went unmarked.

The casino area dominated all. Extensive, with more chandeliers, it was crowded with tables devoted to card playing, gaming wheels, tip baskets, and many other devices dedicated to extracting money from those with the inclination to try their luck.

There were many. Despite the early hour, the Palace was well filled, which led to the conclusion that in Babylon there was no day, no night — only a time for gambling and drinking and the pursuit of any other purpose available within its high-windowed walls.

At least a dozen of the card tables were occupied, no less than four players sitting in on each game. Groups surrounded the chuck-a-luck stand, the faro dealers, the blackjack table; more crowded about a sallow-faced man operating a roulette wheel. A balcony off which led a corridor and that was reached by a stairway curving up from the end of the mahogany bar overlooked the entire operation.

Shawn smiled. As the two Dodge City lawmen had said, a fortune had gone into the building of the Babylon Palace and its adjoining enterprises, but the bread they had cast upon the waters was returning to them tenfold and then some.

He moved away from the entrance, angling across the hard, bare floor toward the bar. A woman turned lazily from the foot of the stairs and raised her dark, full brows questioningly at him.

She was undoubtedly young, attractive, almost beautiful in fact, or could be were she devoid of the rouge and rice powder that layered her face. The yellow dress she wore did little to conceal her well-proportioned body, and the circular, cardboard medallion suspended by a red ribbon about her neck and nestling in the deep valley of her well-developed bosom proclaimed her name to be Jenny.

Starbuck smiled again, waved her off,

noting then with interest that all of the women in sight were equally young and pretty as Frank had said, and that they also wore name tags. McGraw and his partner, Fisher, had matters down to a precise system, it appeared.

Reaching the bar, Shawn took his place near the center of the two dozen or so men lined up before it. A middle-aged man, balding and with round, blue eyes, wearing a white bib apron and a name plate bearing the word *Pete,* eased up to him.

"Yours?"

"Make it rye," Starbuck replied, nodding, and then added, "Pete."

The bartender's expression did not change as he reached down to a shelf under the counter, procured a glass and bottle, and poured the drink.

"Four bits," he said, sliding the thick-bottomed container toward Shawn.

Starbuck reached into a pocket for a coin. Prices were high in Babylon, but he supposed he should have expected it. A man partakes of luxury, he should be willing to shell out for it.

"Keep it all," he said, picking up the glass.

Pete's features responded to that. He nodded, grinned, revealed twin rows of yellowed, uneven teeth.

"Much obliged, Mister — Mister —"

"Starbuck," Shawn supplied, and turned slowly on a heel.

Elbows hooked on the rolled edge of the bar, he glanced out over the broad room. The crowd had increased around the roulette wheel where some fortunate gambler was evidently having a run of good luck. A man with a shock of snow-white hair and wearing a dark suit had settled at one of the pianos and was playing an old war tune. Somewhere upstairs in one of the corridors a woman laughed shrilly.

Two men came through the doorway and paused briefly to stare about as if in search of someone. Smoke, unnoticed earlier, clung to the ceiling in a dense layer, muffling the steady racket and descending gradually as its mass thickened. Eventually it would submerge the glittering chandeliers.

"First time in the Palace?"

At Pete's question Shawn came half around. "First time."

The bartender grinned widely, mopped at the polished surface of the counter with a damp cloth.

"Sure a sight for sore eyes, ain't it?"

"For a fact," Shawn agreed, draining his

glass. "Been here long?"

"Ever since the place was opened. Head bartender for the past year."

"You must've seen a lot of people come and go."

"A hell of a lot more'n I can recollect!"

"I was hoping you might remember one — my brother. Probably looks something like me. Maybe called himself Damon Friend."

Pete ceased his scrubbing, studied Shawn intently. "Face of yours does look familiar. Name don't ring no bells, howsomever. Didn't you say yours was Starbuck?"

Shawn nodded. "His is, too — Ben Starbuck, but he started calling himself Damon Friend. We had a family breakup."

"I see," Pete murmured. After a moment he shook his head. "Wish't I could help, but I can't think of nobody looking like you or answering to either one of them handles. Let me study on it a couple of days . . . You expect to be around for a spell?"

"It's what I've got in mind to do. I was told this would be a good place to look for him."

"The best. We get them all here — good ones and bad ones, heading north, south,

30

east, and west. Could be you'll find your brother somewheres in here right now, upstairs with one of the gals or maybe in there bucking the tiger, was you to look around."

"That's what I aim to do. Be obliged if you'd do some thinking back, see if you can remember."

"I'm remembering —"

At the sound of the familiar, grating voice, Starbuck's jaw clicked shut. Setting the empty glass on the bar, he wheeled. A grimness moved into him as he faced the three men ranged before him, and his memory flipped back to a time in far-distant New Mexico — an attempted stagecoach robbery, an alley behind a saloon in the small settlement of Las Cruces, a stuffy, heat-ridden jail.

Dallman and his friend, the pimple-faced, straw-haired boy he'd called the Kid. Now there was a third partner — a stranger with a scarred chin. The outlaw had promised they would someday meet again. That time was at hand.

4

Only those standing at the bar were aware of the sudden, breathless tension that had descended so abruptly. Elsewhere in the Babylon Palace the whisp of cards, the click of gambling wheels, the mutter of voices, the thump of a piano, continued uninterrupted.

Starbuck leaned back against the mahogany counter, hands hung loosely at his sides, head thrust forward. Dallman, a dark stubble of beard on his broad face, arms crossed, considered him with narrowed eyes.

"I told you I'd be looking you up. I ain't a man to ever forget nothing."

"Maybe this time you should," Starbuck drawled. "Healthier."

"He's a wise one, ain't he?" the scarred stranger commented, doubling his hamlike fists. "Come on, let's take him."

"No big rush, Al," Dallman said. "Like to make this last. I owe this jasper plenty

— me and the Kid. He left us sweating it out in a goddam lousy jail once. Now it's my turn to make him sweat."

Farther along the bar a voice murmured, "Somebody better fetch the marshal."

"Ain't got one," Pete replied. "Elmo quit, rode out more'n a week ago."

Starbuck, a half smile cracking his long lips, stirred. "I'm a bit surprised you're out of that Cruces jail. Seems the law sure slipped up there."

"Law ain't cornered me yet —"

"Day'll come . . . Now, if you've got something on your mind, get on with it. I'm beat and I aim to find myself a bed."

"Sure," Dallman said softly, and reaching out quickly, caught the Kid by the arm and swung him straight at Shawn.

Starbuck jerked aside. The Kid thudded into the long counter, the impact setting up a rattle of glasses and bottles. Lunging forward, Shawn clamped a hand upon that of Dallman as the outlaw drew his gun and smashed a hard right to his jaw.

Al swore and rushed in, arms swinging. Starbuck spun away from the staggered Dallman and took a hard blow in the ribs from the scar-faced man as he fell back.

Al yelled again and crowded in close.

Shawn halted, dropped unconsciously into the cocked stance of a trained boxer drilled into him so deeply by old Hiram Starbuck in the far-gone days on the Muskingum. As Al surged in, Shawn rapped him sharply across the nose with a stinging left that brought a flush of blood, followed with a right to the jaw that cracked like a muleskinner's whip when it connected.

The scarred man halted flat-footed, arms sagging to his sides while a look of pained surprise crossed his features. Shawn touched him with a glance, saw he would have no further problems with him for the next few moments, and pivoted to Dallman. In that same instant the Kid came at him from the left, throwing himself upon his back, wrapping his arms about his waist, and pinning his hands to his body. Immediately Starbuck hunched forward, braced himself on spraddled legs as he sought to remain upright under the Kid's weight.

"Get him! Get him now!"

At the Kid's desperate plea, Shawn swung around, striving to block Dallman with the younger man's body. The outlaw moved in quickly. Fists poised, he was grinning broadly. Shawn took a blow to the belly, jerked his head to one side as he avoided another aimed at his jaw.

"Get him, Hake!" the Kid yelled again.

Whirling, side-stepping, bobbing, Starbuck struggled to dislodge the burden on his back and free his arms. The Kid clung like a leech, his weight refusing to budge. Starbuck winced as Dallman smashed another knotted fist into his ribs, once more managed to duck a second try for his jaw.

Breath was coming hard, and the weight he was supporting was taking toll of his strength. From the tail of his eye he saw Al shaking off the inertia that had gripped him, realized that he would shortly be moving in, getting his licks . . . He realized he must do something fast or he would find himself at the mercy of the three outlaws.

Staggering, he pulled back, came up against one of the bystanders. The man pushed him off, sent him stumbling toward one of the ceiling support pillars as Hake Dallman shouted and stepped closer. But Starbuck had recognized his salvation.

Mustering his strength, he continued on for the column, a foot-square timber of solid oak beneath its coat of paint. He reached it, pivoted fast, smashed the Kid against it. The man yelled in pain and released his locked hands. Starbuck lunged him against the pillar again as Dallman's fists began to pound at him. The load fell from his back, and sucking for wind, he ducked and spun off as Dallman, now sided by Al, crowded in.

Shawn took a half a dozen blows on the arms and shoulders as he stalled to recover breath and balance. The two outlaws were pressing him hard, both grinning their confidence.

Starbuck took a step backward, came up against something rigid. He had collided with a chair. Reaching down, he gripped it by its curved top and swung it at the pair. The chair splintered on Al's head and shoulders, slid off onto Hake Dallman. Both men halted briefly.

But it was long enough for Shawn to get himself squared away, and when the two outlaws had recovered from the interruption and resumed their advance, he was ready.

He caught Dallman with a stiff left to the eyes, danced away, and then, swift as a striking rattler, darted in, tagged the blood-smeared Al with a solid right to the ear.

Both men wheeled, seemingly uncertain of where they were. Shawn rocked Hake with a vicious crack to the head, followed it with an uppercut that missed but skimmed across the man's cheek and drew red.

Al, roaring his rage, bent low and with arms outstretched, big hands spread wide, rushed in. Starbuck waited until the last possible instant, feinted right, and brought down a sledging fist. It struck the outlaw just below the temple and dropped him spread-eagled to the floor.

Sucking for wind, he pivoted to Dallman, who was once again rushing toward him. Beyond the man Shawn could see the Kid. He still lay at the base of the ceiling support, red-smeared features lax, eyes glazed and unseeing. The crowd surrounding them had grown, too, he saw, and the noise coming from the casino area had ceased.

He let Dallman come to him, backing away to lead the man on, to purposely infuriate and draw him in to carelessness. Abruptly Hake took the bait, threw caution aside. Yelling a curse, he plunged forward, arms swinging.

It was the opening Starbuck had been hoping for. As the outlaw crowded in close, he blocked a long, right-handed swing with his left forearm. Dallman rocked back, off balance from the abrupt checking of his momentum, and left himself wide open.

Starbuck's knotted fist, brought up from the knees, caught the man flush on the point of the jaw.

The blow raised Hake Dallman to his toes. He seemed to hang there suspended for a long time, and then he buckled, collapsed to the floor in a heap.

A growl went up behind him. Shawn wheeled, hand dropping to the forty-five on his hip . . . He had had enough. He was tired and had no stomach for further conflict with additional friends of Hake Dallman.

"Reckon three-to-one odds is plenty for any man."

Shawn's eyes halted on the speaker, a burly redhead dressed in ordinary range clothing. He held a cocked six-gun in his freckled hand, had it leveled carelessly at a knot of hard cases who apparently had decided to cut themselves into the fight.

"Now, supposing the four of you back away — keep out of it."

"That's right!" someone in the crowd added. "If you sage-hoppers is looking for a free-for-all, why I reckon some of us'll be glad to oblige!"

The men hung quiet for a long breath, and then the one slightly forward shrugged, turned away. Immediately his companions swung about, and all pushed through the circle of bystanders, headed for a table where they had apparently been sitting.

Starbuck glanced at the outlaws on the floor. Only the Kid was making any effort to gain his feet. Dallman and Al were still out cold and unquestionably finished.

Shawn turned to the redhead as men nearby began to clap him on the back and shout their congratulations. He nodded to the husky rider.

"Thanks . . . I'd like to buy you a drink."

The redhead smiled, holstered his weapon. "It was a pleasure, friend . . . And I'll take that drink. Got myself a table over here."

5

"Name's Starbuck," Shawn said as they settled down, a shot glass of whiskey in hand.

The husky man bobbed his head to the introduction. "Folks mostly call me Red," he replied, the words having the faintly rounded edges of the South to them. "You sure do take on a crowd when you decide to fracas."

"Not my idea," Shawn grinned ruefully, probing a tenderness along his face where he had taken a stiff blow. "One at a time's generally a plenty."

Red shifted his attention to the floor. The crowd had melted, each man returning to whatever had occupied his attention before the interruption. The Kid and Al were upright and helping Hake Dallman to the table where the remainder of their party awaited them.

"Was a plenty for that bunch," Red observed dryly. "What was it all about?"

Starbuck shrugged. "Little trouble I had down in New Mexico. I was there looking for my brother, stumbled onto them. We didn't part friends."

"I gathered that. You say you're looking for a brother?"

"Yeh — Ben, or maybe I ought to call him Damon Friend. Think that's the name he's going by, but I'm not sure. Best bet I'd say is that we probably look alike."

"Probably?" Red echoed, sipping at his drink.

"I haven't seen him in quite a few years. He left home one day after a row with my pa."

"I see. Where's home?"

"Ohio. Farm on the Muskingum River. There's a town there with the same name."

"That where you learned to use your fists? I seen that belt you're wearing —"

"Belonged to pa. He was good at boxing. He could have been a champion, I expect, if he'd wanted it that way. He liked farming more."

"Well, he done a mighty fine job of teaching you, I'll say that!"

"He taught Ben and me both. One way I hope to find him. I know he's put on a couple of exhibition matches, and I'm on the watch for one. You ever see a match?"

41

"Nope, never did . . . Finding him's pretty important to you, I take it."

Starbuck twirled his half-empty glass between a thumb and forefinger. "It is. When pa died, he left a will. He said I had to run Ben down, bring him back home before the estate could be settled . . . It runs to a pretty fair amount of money. I don't get my share until I find him."

"I thought you said they parted in a row?"

"They did, only pa was sorry afterwards. He kept hoping Ben would come back — right up to the day he died. Ben was sort of his favorite, I suppose."

"And you was your ma's fair-haired boy."

Shawn grinned. "Guess so."

"Same in my family, only was the other way around."

"You got a brother you're looking for, too?"

"Nope. He's dead now. Me — I'm just drifting."

Starbuck continued to toy with his glass. One drink had been sufficient to satisfy him; he had ordered a second from Pete only to be sociable.

"I sometimes think that's where Ben is — dead — and that I'm riding trails for nothing."

"Ain't you ever got close enough to even see him?"

"Nope. Once or twice I've hit a town where somebody who might've been him was just there — but being sure is always only a guess. Like Las Cruces — where I bumped into Dallman and the Kid. A man had put on a boxing exhibition there. Description could have fit Ben. The boxing part, that fit, too. Another thing, the man called himself Damon Friend.

"One of the favorite stories that my ma — she was a schoolteacher — used to read to Ben and me when we were kids was about Damon and Pythias — you know, the two good friends —"

Red nodded. "I remember it."

"Well, it would've been natural for Ben to take some of the name, use it."

"Maybe, but if it was only a family fuss, why would he change? Why wouldn't he just call himself Ben Starbuck?"

"It was part of the squabble — or maybe I ought to say it was a result of it. When he left, Ben was boiling mad. Said he was changing his name, that he didn't want to ever hear it again, long as he lived . . . Knowing Ben, I'm pretty sure he stuck to his word."

Red finished off his drink, stared into the

empty shot glass. "And you been hunting him ever since."

"Only since pa died, of course, but seems like I've been at it all my life."

"Way it adds up," Red said, leveling his cold, blue eyes at Shawn, "that's about what you'll likely end up doing. This is one hell of a big country to find one man in."

"I realized that a time back. Figured it would be a cinch at first. Thought I knew right where Ben would go and hightailed it for that place. I was right — or partly so. Ben had been there, only he'd moved on."

"And you've been in the saddle ever since."

"Except when I have to pull up, work a spell to get some traveling cash . . . What brings you here?"

Red's thick shoulders stirred. "Oh, just to see the elephant, I reckon . . . Sure is some layout."

"For a fact. Never heard of Babylon being here until yesterday when I was in Dodge. The marshal and his jailer told me about it. Said it was one place where my chances of running into him or finding out something about him would be good."

"They were right. Expect it's true what they say about every man in the country riding by here sooner or later."

Starbuck looked out over the room. The crowd had increased, and smoke was now a wavering blanket hovering in a layer that was even with the chandeliers. The table Dallman and his friends had occupied was deserted, the outlaws either having departed or moved into and become lost in the throng milling about in the gambling area.

"You run into any leads yet?"

"Only one I've talked to about it is Pete, the bartender, and you. Pete couldn't remember, but he said he'd think about it."

"Try the women. They always remember a man."

"Aim to talk to them . . . Sure some fine-looking ones here."

"They're the big drawing card. Hear there ain't a one of them over twenty years old — except old Bessie. She runs the café."

"Looks like this McGraw and his partner had the right idea. Never saw so much gambling and the like in one place before in all my life. It go on around the clock?"

"They close down for the mornings. They can damn sure afford to. Place is a mint. Considering the size of it and all the fancy decorating and equipment, it cost McGraw and Fisher a pretty penny, but

45

I'm betting they've got it all back by now."

"Takes money to make money," Shawn murmured.

"Ain't no doubt of that — and speaking of the ramrods, we're about to be visited by one."

Following Red's glance, Shawn saw a dark, well-dressed man with the immobile features of a gambler moving toward them from the bar. He carried a bottle in one hand, a glass in the other.

"Which one — Fisher or McGraw?"

"Bart Fisher," Red replied. "McGraw ain't around."

Fisher, lips set to a fixed smile beneath a carefully trimmed mustache, stepped up to the table, nodding genially.

"I just want to offer my congratulations," he said, looking at Starbuck. "The way you handled those toughs was a caution. I'm Bart Fisher, half owner of Babylon. I'd like to treat you to a drink."

The gambler's voice was cool, low, bespoke an education. Shawn nodded. "Sure, why not? You know Red?"

Fisher settled onto a chair, glanced at the redhead. "I've seen him around."

"I'm mighty glad he was today," Starbuck said. "Got to admit I'd had about enough."

"I can't say that it showed," Fisher replied with a short laugh as he filled his glass along with the redhead's and the partly empty one in front of Shawn. Putting the bottle aside, he lifted his drink in salute. "Here's how!"

Starbuck downed his liquor, then returned his glass to the table and covered it with his hand. He shifted his attention to the gambler, feeling the man's sharp eyes drilling into him.

"I don't think I've ever seen you in the Palace before."

"No, first time."

"Pete tells me you're hunting for a brother."

Shawn bobbed his head. "I have been for quite a time. I'm hoping he'll turn up here — if he hasn't already."

"Odds are all for it." Fisher refilled his glass, looked questioningly at Starbuck and then at Red. Both declined. "Where you from, mostly?"

"Just about any place you can mention. Home was in Ohio."

Fisher eased back into his chair. "Then you're not tied down to any one place?"

"No — not specially."

"Then maybe you'd be interested in a job."

Starbuck frowned. "Here?"

Bart Fisher smiled his artificial smile. "Yeh, here. We're needing a marshal."

6

Shawn, surprised, remained silent. Old Hiram Starbuck, in setting forth the requirement that his younger son first find his brother before the estate could be divided, had neglected to provide funds for the search. Thus Shawn, periodically, when cash ran low, was compelled to stop and seek work to replenish his capital.

He was not in that particular position at the moment, just having come off a job in Texas, but there was an attraction in Bart Fisher's offer; he intended to hang around for a while anyway, and by assuming the lawman chore, he could for once since it all began be searching and earning at the same time. But it could prove to be quite a task — keeping law and order in a place like Babylon.

"Take that as a compliment, Mr. Fisher —"

"Bart —"

"Bart . . . What happened to the marshal you had?"

"Elmo? He was a good man, but he got himself involved with one of the girls, and they ran off together. Last I heard was that they got married in Dodge and he went to work for some cattle outfit . . . You aren't thinking of marriage, are you?"

Shawn grinned, shook his head. "Not for quite a spell."

The desire, the need for a home, a wife, and a family had come upon him several times, and often the opportunity for such had presented itself, but he had quickly put it from his mind; he could plan no life of his own until the matter of finding Ben was concluded.

"That's good. We don't want any more Elmos around. Oh, you're free to get friendly with the girls! No rule against that — just don't get yourself sold on one of them. We've got twenty-three of them in the Palace, and you'll have your choice any time. Living quarters and meals go along with the deal, too."

Starbuck glanced at Red. The man was looking off toward the gambling area, seemingly uninterested in the conversation.

"What about a deputy? Any need for one?"

The co-owner of Babylon poured himself another drink. His shoulders stirred. "Never had one before. We get all kinds here — good, bad, and worse — but one badge-toter has always been able to do the job. Think, perhaps, it's the place itself. Being plenty high-class, they sort of hold themselves in and don't break loose like they might in some ordinary ragtag saloon.

"And that's the way we expect our marshal to keep it. The brawlers have to be put outside. That ruckus you had with those men today is the first that's broken loose inside in months — and it wouldn't have happened if we'd had a lawman on the job.

"The badge is legal, by the way. We've been given authority by the state to appoint our own marshal, run a jail, and hold court. Your authority is good, so there's no need to feel that you're a jackleg lawman."

Shawn considered Fisher's words. "When do you want me to start — if I take it?"

"Immediately — tonight if possible. Not later than tomorrow."

"What about your partner?"

"It'll be all right with Amos. He's away on business, but what I do is always jake with him. We've got a big investment here, and we've got to protect it."

"I can understand that. Does the job

51

mean looking after everything else around here, too — the stores and all?"

Bart Fisher nodded. "Amos and I own it all, every square foot. We bought the land, built the buildings, put in the stores and businesses. We hire people to run them for us — that way we've got no competition, not in anything. Anybody wants to buck us, they'll have to set up outside the town limits, which covers a square mile."

"Sure got it all your own way," Red murmured, coming into the conversation.

"That's how it should be. We put up the cash to build Babylon. We're entitled to a big return on our money."

"I'm not saying you ain't, but I'm bleeding for them in places like Dodge who don't have it your way. Heard when I was there that there's nineteen saloons and only twelve hundred people in the town. Bar owners there sure ain't going to get rich."

Irritation stirred through Fisher as he considered the redhead. "It's the truth, and you'll find just about the same situation everywhere else. It's the reason Amos and I decided to do it this way — build our own town so's we could control it." Abruptly the gambler turned to Shawn. "What's your answer? Job pays a hundred a month and keep. You want it or not?"

Starbuck shrugged. "I done a time as a deputy sheriff once. I don't expect this will be much different."

Fisher extended his hand, enclosed that of Shawn. "We've got a deal. Like for you to start tonight if you can."

"No problem."

"Fine. The marshal's office is open. You'll find your badge in the desk drawer, and I'm officially swearing you in as of now. Living quarters are off the jail. Put your horse in the stable next door . . . Now, anything else you want to know?"

"About covers it unless you've got some special orders."

"None," the gambler said, rising. "I'll leave it up to you to arrange your rounds — bearing in mind that the biggest part of your time is to be spent inside the Palace. Just keep things in hand, that's what we're interested in — but do it without hurting business."

Starbuck gave that a moment's thought. "You mean you don't want any arrests made?"

"Not necessarily. I'll leave that up to you, and if it's something that needs a trial, Amos is the judge. He'll hold court and pass sentence . . . Oh, maybe there is one thing I ought to tell you — keep an eye on the Flophouse."

"Flophouse?"

"Place out back," Red explained. "Like a bunkhouse. Man goes broke in here, he can throw his bedroll down in there — no charge, free for nothing."

"Simply good business," Fisher said stiffly. "We figure it's better to give a man a place to sleep than have him go to the hotel, rent a room, and then not have the money to pay for it. Only one rule: We won't stand for any gambling there — not any kind. If a man's got some cash, we want it spent in here, not forked over to some two-bit cardsharp."

"Which boils down to a man's being welcome to spread his blanket in the Flophouse if he's dead broke," Shawn said.

"Exactly," Fisher replied. "Be seeing you later."

The gambler moved off toward the bar. Starbuck watched him hand the bottle of liquor, apparently his own private stock used for special occasions, to one of the bartenders and head on into the crowded casino area.

"You need a job that bad?" Red asked in a disgusted tone of voice.

Shawn turned to face the husky man.

"No," he said quietly. "Fact is, I don't need a job at all, but since I figure to hang around for a spell, I might as well get paid for doing it."

Red grinned. "Makes sense," he admitted, his manner changing. "Fellow has a chance to get money out of this place would be a fool not to grab it . . . Sure about the only way you'll ever see any of their cash."

"I was trying to line you up for a little of it — as my deputy."

"Not me. Be glad to pitch in, give you a hand if it's ever needful, but I ain't wearing no star."

"It don't hurt much . . . How about bunking in with me? Expect my quarters'll be big enough for two."

"No thanks — again. Got myself a good room in the hotel. As soon stay put."

"Suit yourself, but if you go busted, offer stands. Be better than moving into the Flophouse."

The redhead smiled, nodded. "Appreciate that."

Starbuck pushed back from the table. "I think I'd better see to my horse and move my blanket roll into my new home. What time you aim to eat?"

"Six o'clock or thereabouts."

Shawn drew himself upright, bobbed his head. "Fine. Meet you at the restaurant."

It was not until Starbuck had reached, and was passing through, the ornate doorway that the realization came to him; Red had never, during their conversation, stated his real name. Such could only mean there was a reason why he wished his identity to remain hidden.

There was nothing unusual in that, however. Likely a third of the men in the Babylon Palace at that very moment were using a name other than the one they were christened with — and it was neither polite nor safe to dig into the reason why.

And Shawn had no intentions of doing so. He liked the husky redhead, and while he had encountered and become associated with many other men during his wandering across the land, Red was the first to strike so deep a responsive chord within him. He could furnish himself with no good explanation as to why; certainly he had known other men for longer periods of time, had even undergone higher stress and weathered greater danger with some, but he had never permitted any of them to become a close friend.

With Red it was different. It seemed they had been acquainted for years although the actual length of their friendship barely bridged an hour. Starbuck frowned as a thought came to him: Could it be that the redhead reminded him of old Hiram? Of Ben?

7

There was little noticeable difference between day and night in Babylon. The wheels of chance continued to whirr and click, the dice to roll. The card tables remained occupied while the women plied their trade and the barmen served their drinks as sundown came and darkness clothed the land.

Shawn, his horse stabled, pleased with his quarters — which were separate from, but connected to, his office in the jail — and wearing the badge of his calling, stood at the foot of the stairway in the noisy, glittering Palace and marveled at the shifting, surging crowd.

He had expected to see a decrease in the number of men at the ending of day. The exact opposite appeared to be true. Those already present seemed uninterested in departing, or in even taking time out for a meal, while a steady, if thin stream of newcomers continued to arrive. It was as if each man feared the days of the fabulous Palace were numbered and was frantically determined to partake of its offerings as fully as possible before Armageddon prevailed.

Moving off the lower step of the stair, Shawn cruised slowly through the throng, speaking to those acknowledging him, searching the faces of all. Occasionally he would pause, and if someone chose to engage him in conversation, he fell into the exchange willingly — and eventually brought up the subject of his missing brother.

He learned nothing of value, however, but such dismayed him little. Many previous disappointments had hardened him to possibilities, and he had come to accept failure with a brief shrug of his broad shoulders. That he would find Ben when he found him was a philosophy aptly suited to the situation, and he left it at that.

A fight broke out at the blackjack table near the middle of the evening. Two riders in disagreement over some personal matter and deciding to settle it where they stood squared off. Starbuck stepped between them before the first blow was struck and, taking each by an arm, propelled them into the street.

The desire for combat ended there. The two men, scowling darkly, singled out their horses at the rack, mounted, and swung west on the road that led to Raton Pass and New Mexico.

The disturbance created no more than a ripple in the Palace's swirling existence. Shawn's re-entry into the building was noted only by Red, who was again at his same table near the end of the bar where he was content to nurse a drink in solitude. Favoring Starbuck with a faintly derisive smile, he nodded his approval nevertheless as the tall rider passed by.

Minutes later there was a dispute at one of the poker tables. Fisher beckoned hurriedly to Shawn over the heads of the men crowded about, and he moved in quickly. At his appearance belligerence faded from the manner of the narrow-faced player involved, and the matter was settled. The mere presence of a lawman in the Palace did much to keep things on an even keel, it seemed, and Starbuck reckoned that such was as it should be.

Moving on, Shawn turned his steps toward the bar and then paused. Two men standing beyond one of the faro tables caught his attention. Both looked familiar, and then he realized they were part of the gang that had been with Hake Dallman. Evidently all had not left Babylon after the encounter. It could mean more trouble later on.

He discarded his intention to return to the stair from which he had a good, overall view of the establishment's activities and pushed on through the crowd looking for Dallman himself and others of his party. After an hour or so he gave it up. Either they were not present or they were aware of his interest and were skillfully avoiding him.

Around midnight he had a cup of black coffee in a room behind the bar with Pete and one of the dealers. A small kitchen had been set up where light snacks could be had without going outside the Palace to the café.

"Pretty good night," Pete said. Then remembering, he added, "Marshal, this here's Ollie Cates. Works the tables . . . Ollie, the new marshal's name is Shawn Starbuck."

Cates was a quiet-faced man with a pinched mouth. He took Starbuck's hand into his own, squeezed it limply.

"Shawn? Sounds Indian," he observed with no particular interest.

"It is," Starbuck replied. "My ma once

taught some kids of the Shawnee tribe — she was a teacher. Took the name from that."

Cates bobbed his head. "Didn't think you looked much Indian."

Shawn sipped at his cup of the strong, black liquid and listened as Pete explained to the dealer his search for Ben. When he had finished, Cates shrugged his thin shoulders.

"Hell, I don't pay no mind to the suckers I'm dealing to. Just faces, that's all they are to me — and they all look alike. If I ever hear that name, however, I'll remember and let you know. Pretty good at names."

Two of the girls came into the room, one a plump brunette in a shiny green dress and wearing a tag with Anna printed upon it, the other a slim Mexican with large, doelike eyes and smooth, dusky skin that glowed in the lamplight. She was called Chica.

Recalling Pete's earlier words, Starbuck asked them about Ben, or Damon Friend. The Mexican girl shook her head, but Anna, lacing her coffee with a generous portion of whiskey, which she poured from a flask affixed to her lower thigh by a garter, thought she remembered a Damon Friend, but she wasn't sure. It had been a

62

long time ago — possibly a year.

"I don't recollect him looking much like you," she said. "Seems he was a short man, but if I ain't all mixed up in my thinking, the cowpoke with him called him Friend. It could have been his name, or maybe that puncher was just saying friend — like some men do instead of saying mister."

"There anybody else around here who might remember him?" Starbuck asked.

Anna refilled her cup, fortified the coffee once more with liquor. "Could be. Most of these johns hang around a few days till they're either all caught up or busted flat before they ride out. If you want, I'll —"

"Marshal —" a voice called from the doorway. "Got some bad trouble out here."

Immediately Shawn wheeled and returned to the casino area. A circle had formed in the center. Two men standing an arm's length apart, hands hanging close to their guns, faced a third who was regarding both with steady intent. There was a hard, bright glint in his eyes, and the flush of liquor heightened his color. He, too, was poised, half bent, his splayed fingers hovering near the butt of the pistol thonged to his leg.

"Keep out of this," he warned softly as

63

Starbuck pushed into the cleared space. "They been crowding me. Aim to oblige them."

"All right — but not in here," Shawn said coolly. "You want to settle something, go outside. Don't want anybody else in here hurt."

The gunman's head barely moved. "No —"

Starbuck's muscles tightened. Here was real trouble. Brawling cowhands, drunks, and discomfited card players were one thing — a gunslinger out to even a score was something else. A half a dozen bystanders could fall in an exchange of bullets.

The Babylon Palace had paused, become silent awaiting the outcome. The only sound was the distant barking of a dog. Shawn gauged the two men standing side by side. Their features were drawn, set, and the flicker of uncertainty was in their eyes. He had nothing to fear from them. Cornered by the gunman, they would like nothing better than to back away and leave.

Moving slowly in beside the coiled figure of the gunslinger, Starbuck made a final try. "I'm telling you once more — forget it."

"The hell with you . . . I'm going to —"

Shawn drew his weapon swiftly and swung it hard at the side of the man's head. The barrel struck with a meaty thud. The gunman wilted, sprawled onto the floor.

A heavy sigh went up from the crowd, and the two trail hands, their frozen features breaking into smiles of relief, nodded crisply to Starbuck, turned on their heels, and hurried toward the door. Shawn, tension draining from his taut body, holstered his pistol and stepped back. Bart Fisher stepped into the cleared area and beckoned to several men near the bar.

"Take him to the hotel and put him to bed," he directed, pointing to the gunman. "Tell Carlton the room's to be no charge."

The gambler moved back a step to allow the men to close in and pick up the unconscious man, then swung his attention to Starbuck.

"As neat a job of buffaloing as I've ever seen," he said, smiling. "Where'd you learn that?"

"Dodge City. I saw the deputy there handle a man that way yesterday."

Fisher bobbed his head in approval. "Most effective. I want you to know I think you're doing a fine job."

The gambler turned away and walked off

among the tables. Shawn glanced around. Bystanders were staring at him thoughtfully, silently, and he knew they were forming their opinions of him — opinions that would set him apart, cause them to withdraw and leave him strictly alone. But it was to be expected. He had had a time as a lawman, known beforehand the loneliness that went with the calling.

Near midnight he began to feel the drag of the late hour. He had been up since sunrise and in the saddle all of the day; weariness was at last beginning to catch up with him. He made a second trip to the kitchen, deserted at that moment, and helped himself to another cup of the strong coffee.

A shot of whiskey added to the portion would have been of help, but there was none handy, and he disliked the idea of going to the bar for it.

The girl called Jenny entered while he was draining the last of his cup and smiled tiredly at him. He nodded, filled the china container she picked up, and took advantage of the moment to ask her about Ben. She could give him no help but, like the others, promised to ask around and do what she could.

"If he ain't been here yet, he'll show up

66

some day," she said as he started for the door.

Once again in the casino, Shawn circulated through the noisy gathering until he found Bart Fisher.

"It's been a long day," he said, drawing the gambler aside. "I'm going to make the rounds once more and turn in."

A frown crossed Fisher's face, and then his shoulders lifted, fell. "Suit yourself. Anything comes up I can't handle, I'll send for you."

"You do that," Starbuck replied dryly, and turning away, cut back through the crowd.

Fisher expected him to stay on the job for the entire night, he supposed, but he was in no condition to do so. It didn't matter. If the gambler didn't like it, he knew what he could do with the job.

Red was no longer at his table, he noticed as he made his way to the street. He would see him at breakfast in the morning. Stepping off the Palace porch, he crossed along the fronts of the stores facing the open ground, checking the doors and peering inside. Following a like procedure, he investigated the alley entrances, found all secure, and satisfied, sought out his quarters, crawling onto the bed without troubling to remove any of his clothing other than his boots.

He had scarcely closed his eyes, it seemed, when he roused to a hand shaking his shoulder. He sat up quickly, faced Fisher and several other men from the Palace.

"I've been robbed!" the gambler cried in an agitated voice. "There's better'n twenty thousand dollars missing!"

8

Starbuck came to his feet, stared groggily at Fisher. Through the window beyond the men he could see sunlight, realized he had actually been asleep for hours.

"How'd they manage it?" he asked, stamping into his boots and reaching for his gun belt. "A holdup?"

"No — hid in the office where we keep the safe. When the cashier went back to stash the take in the safe — he does that every three or four hours so we don't have too much cash laying around — they were waiting. They knew what they were doing. They held off until he opened the safe, then cold-cocked him. Took what he was carrying along with another sack they found inside."

Starbuck pulled on his hat and started for the door. "This man you call the cashier, he able to talk?"

"He was still out when we found him —

about ten minutes ago. Could be he's come to by now."

Walking briskly, they left the jail and hurried to the Palace. The cashier, an elderly, balding man, had regained consciousness and was sitting in a chair, a drink in one hand while he held a wet compress to the side of his head. He nodded weakly to Shawn.

"Sure nailed me good, Marshal," he said.

"Glad you're alive. How many of them were there?"

"Two was all I seen."

"Know them?"

"Nope, leastwise not by name, but I can tell you who they are."

Fisher swore impatiently. "What's that mean? You said you didn't know them."

"What I'm meaning is that I've seen them around the place. They've been hanging around two, maybe three days. Fact is, they was two of them four that started to horn in on that ruckus you had, Marshal, when you first come in."

Dallman's bunch. The pair he had noticed in the Palace earlier that evening, probably. Hake and the Kid, along with the rest of the gang, had likely been waiting outside to lend a hand in the event the two were forced to shoot their way out.

"Think I know the ones you're talking about," he said. "Remember seeing them here. Any idea which way they rode off?"

"South," Bart Fisher said promptly. "They'd head for Brewer's Flat."

Starbuck glanced at the gambler. "That a town?"

Fisher nodded. "Outlaw hangout — in the Indian Territory panhandle. Unclaimed land — no law there."

One of the saloon girls came into the office and crossed to the gambler. "The money's not all they got. They took Dolly and Jenny with them."

The gambler swore deeply. "Took or went?"

The girl fingered her name tag. Hallie, it read. "Took, I'd guess. Their things are still in their room."

"Kidnapped them," Pete said firmly. "They wouldn't have throwed in with a bunch of crud like that bunch. Anyways, Jenny wouldn't. Maybe that Dolly, but not Jenny."

"They probably had it all planned out," Fisher said, rubbing at his chin nervously. "Hung around here getting it lined up. Figured it was a good time to pull it — us having no marshal. Then when you took on the job, that forced them to act this morning — while you were sleeping. Expect you to go after them, Starbuck. I want the money and the women, both, brought back here."

Shawn smiled. "I figured you would. How far is this Brewer's Flat?"

"Short day's ride to the south and east —"

"I know where it is," Red said from the doorway. "You willing, I'll ride with you."

Starbuck swung to the redhead. "I'll be obliged to you."

"Take more than two men," Fisher said, scowling. "Posse would be more like it."

"Never get in there," Red pointed out. "The whole place would turn out and fight. You called it right — it's an outlaw hangout, nobody else welcome."

Fisher shifted his attention back to Shawn. "Well, it's up to you. I can organize a posse mighty quick if you say the word."

"Best just the two of us go, like Red says. Chances'll be better that way."

The gambler made a gesture with his hands. "You're running it. Only thing I'm interested in is getting back the twenty thousand and the two women. When are you leaving?"

"Right now," Starbuck replied, and moved for the door.

★ ★ ★

It was late in the afternoon when they drew to a halt at the mouth of a deep wash, one they had followed for a good hour through a land of ragged buttes, white sand, and low hills covered with thin grass, thistle, and yucca.

"That's it," Red said, pointing to a collection of squalid huts, a corral, and one fair-size building a quarter mile ahead.

"It's more like a camp than a town," Shawn commented, eyes sweeping the area, seeking a route of unobserved approach.

"That's about all it is. The big building's the saloon and store. Run by an old hide hunter named Buffalo Brady. He rents out the shacks to anybody that can pay for hiding out."

"Law's not after him?"

"Not far as I know. No need for him to get himself crossways with it. Makes a good living doing what he's doing."

"The land's pretty flat — open," Starbuck said. "It's not going to be easy moving in unless we wait for dark, and Dallman and his bunch could be gone by then — if they rode in to start with."

"They'll be there," the redhead replied. "Be the one spot they'd figure was safe —

and that's what they'd be looking for after robbing a place like the Babylon Palace."

Shawn nodded. "The closest and the safest."

"Far as getting in, it won't be no big chore from the other side. Lot of brush and sandy washes. Can work in easy without ever being spotted."

Starbuck swung his gaze to the redhead. "You been here before?"

"Once," the man replied, and touching his horse with his rowels, he led the way back out of the arroyo.

They circled wide, keeping behind the hills until they were on the flank directly opposite the camp. Pulling to a stop in a scatter of junipers, they dismounted and, picketing their mounts, hunched low and began to move toward the settlement.

A short time later, in a fringe of dense brush, Red dropped a hand on Shawn's shoulder and paused. Starbuck raised his head cautiously. Brewer's Flat was no more than a stone's throw away.

He could see clearly the weather-beaten structure that served as a combination general store and saloon. Likely Buffalo Brady maintained his living quarters there, also. On either side were the shacks, some small, others a bit larger, but all in the same sad state of disrepair. Immediately to their right and on their side of the clearing were the remnants of what had once been a stable. Only portions of the walls, some of the stalls, and the roof, one end sagging to the ground, remained.

"We can set up a watch from in there," Red suggested, "and see what's going on. First thing we've got to do is find out which shack the bunch has moved into."

Starbuck signified his agreement, and together they dropped back, placed the crumbling old barn between themselves and the occupied buildings, and worked their way into it. Crawling through the litter, they gained the front and settled in behind one of the stall partitions that afforded them a view.

There were more shacks than Shawn had first thought, and Buffalo Brady's store building, while of unpainted, rough timbers, appeared much more sturdy at closer range. Judging from what he could see through the small, dust-filmed windows, Brady also carried a pretty fair stock of merchandise. To the far right of the place a corral could now be seen. There were a dozen or more horses dozing in the late sunlight.

"You got any plan for how we're getting

this job done?" Red asked, stretching out. "There's seven of them, and we can figure on about twice that many others boiling out of their holes to give them a hand when things bust loose."

"Only way it can be done is getting Dallman and his bunch cut off from the rest so's we can move in on them."

"They'll be in one of the shacks — that makes them cut off. Still liable to be one hell of a to-do when we try to take them."

"I know that," Starbuck murmured, his eyes on the distant hills, that were slowly changing color with the lowering of the sun.

Perhaps it would have been better to bring in more men as Bart Fisher had suggested, but he guessed the problem would have been the same; there would still have been a shoot-out and killings, and Buffalo Brady's outlaws, holed up inside the shacks and the saloon, would have had the advantage.

The solution was to locate Dallman, move in quietly, and try to overcome him and his followers without gunfire. Thus all could be accomplished without alerting the remainder of the settlement.

"There's your man now," Red said quietly, pulling himself to his knees.

76

Shawn threw his glance toward the saloon. Hake Dallman, a box of what appeared to be groceries in his hands, and the scarred-chin Al, carrying two quart bottles of whiskey, were coming out onto the store's landing.

They paused briefly. Dallman said something, after which both laughed, and then together they stepped down onto the hardpack fronting the building and started leisurely toward the row of shacks at the lower end of the camp.

"Be the last one," Red muttered hopefully. "Make it easy — for once."

9

It was not to be. Starbuck and Red, crouched inside the old barn, watched as Hake Dallman and Al turned into the largest of the houses standing at the edge of the clearing — one near the center of the row and some distance from the end structure.

The redhead swore softly. "Just can't have no luck," he grumbled.

Shawn made no answer, simply watched the outlaws mount the sagging square of boards that served as a porch for the shack and cross over. Immediately the door swung in and they disappeared. Starbuck had a moment's glimpse into the structure — a table, chairs, shadowy figures clustered around — and then the panel slammed into place.

He settled back. "Nothing we can do now until dark."

"For sure. What then?"

"Get inside — take them by surprise.

Only scheme I've got."

"Have to be a surprise, that's for damn sure. We can't do no shooting, either. Trigger one bullet and we'll have the whole camp down on our necks."

"I realize that. You happen to know whether that shack has a back door?"

The redhead nodded. "They all do. Opens up so's a man can get to the out-house."

"That makes it some easier. One of us will take the front, the other the back. We step inside quick, both at the same time. Big help for us is that they won't be expecting company."

Red grinned wryly. "You remembering what I said — that there's seven of them, along with two women?"

Starbuck shrugged. "I just hope it's no worse than that. Could be there was some-body already in the shack waiting for them when they got here."

"Odds sure don't count for much with you!"

"Maybe, but seems to me the odds are always wrong — so much so that it's got me in the habit of figuring a way to even them up a bit sort of without thinking about it. Like you were saying a while ago, nothing works out easy."

Red hawked, spat into the dust, and then glanced at the sun, now low in the west. "That star you're wearing, it important enough to make you barge right into that nest of rattlesnakes?"

"I was hired to do a job. This is part of the job."

"But trying to corner seven gunnies and take them back over the trail to Babylon — that's really buckin' for the graveyard!"

"I don't aim to take them back. I'm only after the money and the two women. Be stretching luck too far if we tried anything else. Plan's to move in, tie and gag them, and get out of here before the rest of the camp knows what happened."

Red sighed. "I'm glad to hear that. I thought maybe you had in mind to take the whole bunch back and hold yourself a trial."

"It would be the thing to do if there was some way. Dallman won't drop it here, and the best place for him and the rest would be behind bars somewhere. But we can't handle it . . . You got any rope in your gear?"

"Lasso."

"Let's get it. I want to cut it up into three-or-four-foot lengths."

"My rope?"

Shawn grinned at the redhead's pained tone. "I'll see the town of Babylon buys you a new one. We got to have things all set to tie that bunch up with once we're inside. We can make gags out of stuff we'll find laying around."

Red turned, started for the brush. "Think I'll move the horses a mite closer, too. Won't hurt to have them a little handier."

Shawn nodded. "Just so they won't be seen."

The husky man paused. "What about something for the women to ride?"

Starbuck glanced to the distant corral. Getting from that point was out of the question. "I expect they'll have to ride double with us."

Red gave that thought. "Be all right, I reckon, long as there ain't half the town at our heels when we leave here."

"Aim to be sure there's not," Shawn replied, and watched his friend move off through the rubble.

Near sunset two riders came into the camp. They rode straight to Buffalo Brady's store, dismounted, and entered. A short time later they reappeared, evidently having made satisfactory arrangements, and led their horses to the corral where they turned them loose with the others. That done, they retraced their steps to the saloon.

Other than the newcomers, and with the exception of Dallman and his followers, there had been no signs of life in Brewer's Flat. It would seem that it was customary for tenants to stay under cover even while the protective wing of Brady was spread over them.

The last of the sun's golden flare faded in the west, and darkness, cool and hushed, fell over the land. A light wind sprang up, rustling the dead leaves and stirring the brush. A man came out of the store and, trailed by a rangy hound, walked to the corral where he forked a quantity of hay to the animals. Both he and the dog then disappeared in the shadows stretching out from the rear of the shacks.

Shawn rose to his feet, gathered up a share of the rope lengths they had prepared, and glanced at the house occupied by Hake Dallman and his crowd. Lamplight now glowed in its windows. The shack to its right was yet dark, but the one on the opposite side, as well as the saloon and several others in the upper area, were also lit up.

"Let's go," Starbuck said, and turning,

doubled back toward the lower end of the clearing.

Keeping low, they crossed well below the last shack and came into the irregular line from the rear. Paying scant attention to the first, they moved in to the larger house. At once the sound of voices came to them; working their way to a window, they peered in.

The small amount of furniture that had graced the room had been pushed aside. A blanket covered the floor, and the outlaws, in a circle upon it, were engaged in a game of poker. Stacks of currency and piles of coins before each attested to the varying luck of each player. The split of the Palace's twenty thousand dollars had evidently already been made.

The bottles of whiskey, near empty, were close by, and the men, seeking greater comfort, had removed their boots and laid their gun belts on a table. The woman called Jenny watched from a chair placed against a wall; Dolly, crouched beside Al and leaning upon his shoulder, was showing a more avid interest in the game.

Red touched Shawn on the arm and pointed to the adjacent door, indicating he would make his entrance through it. Starbuck nodded.

"Give me time to reach the front," he whispered.

"I'll count to thirty," the redhead murmured.

Shawn moved off, hunched low and walking hurriedly but quietly, mentally taking up the count so that he would throw back the door and perfect an entry at the identical moment as Red.

He reached the corner of the shack at fifteen, gave the open ground to either side a quick scanning, and stepped up onto the landing. Drawing his pistol, he paused there, ticking off the seconds. Someone inside cursed angrily, and down in Buffalo Brady's saloon a woman began to sing in a high, unsteady voice. He hadn't given it thought, but evidently Brady spared no effort in providing conveniences for his customers — even to the point of female companionship.

Twenty-eight . . . Twenty-nine . . . Thirty. . . .

Starbuck raised his leg, drove his booted foot against the door, and sent it crashing inward. As he plunged into the smoky, stale-smelling confines of the room, the back entrance burst wide, also. Red leaped into view.

"Your hands up — all of you!" Starbuck barked in a harsh voice.

10

A scream burst from Dolly's lips. Starbuck kicked the door shut with his heel as Hake Dallman leaped upright. The outlaw clawed for his hip, then remembered suddenly that he was not wearing his gun, that it was on the table.

Shawn lunged at the outlaw, swung his pistol. It caught Hake on the forehead and drove him to his knees. In that same fragment of time the other men jerked back, began to scramble to their feet. Red lashed out with his weapon, clubbed the nearest, and drove his foot into the face of another reaching for him.

The smoky room was filled with the sounds of thrashing bodies, cursing, of men heaving for breath. Hands gripped Starbuck's legs. He swung a balled fist at the dark head at his knees, winced as his knuckles came in contact with flesh and bone. He felt the man's grip slack off, saw the dark head loll to one side.

It was Al, he noted, and spun to grab the Kid struggling to reach the guns on the table. His fingers missed their objective as one of the outlaws butted into him, knocking him off balance.

The Kid, pistol in hand, wheeled. Red surged forward. His arms encircled the young outlaw and crushed the weapon into the Kid's body. There was a muffled explosion. The Kid jolted violently. His mouth popped open as his eyes spread wide, and then he buckled.

Red, tearing the weapon from the Kid's grasp, shoved the limp body at the confused milling in front of him and stepped back. The dead outlaw fell upon one body, slid off, and come to rest across the still-conscious Dallman.

An abrupt hush, broken only by the harsh wheezing of the men sucking for wind, settled over the room. Smoke drifted lazily about, the odor sharpened by the smell of the Kid's smoldering shirt, set on fire by the closeness of the gunshot.

The outlaws, faced by Starbuck on one side, Red on the other, cowed by the sudden death of the Kid, settled back, their hard eyes staring up into the muzzles of the pistols pointed at them.

"Anybody else got a notion?" the redhead asked softly.

There was no response. Shawn, worried not only about the gunshot but Dolly's piercing scream as well, backed to the door. With his free hand he opened it a narrow distance and looked out into the clearing. There was no one on the hardpack. Evidently both sounds had gone unnoticed.

Closing the door, he centered his eyes on the outlaws. "On your bellies — quick!" he ordered, and as the men began to comply, he shifted his attention to the women. "Get that money collected — every dime of it. Put it in that flour sack."

Jenny came forward at once and began to pick up the scattered currency and coins. Dolly, pressed flat against the wall, did not move. Shawn shook his head at her in warning.

"Don't yell again — unless you want to get hurt."

She only stared at him from round, shocked eyes. Evidently she had never before been in such proximity to violence and death. He turned then to assist Red, working steadily at binding the wrists of the outlaws behind their backs and connecting them to a loop of rope encircling their ankles.

With the two of them at it, the task was finished quickly. Starbuck jerked a rag from a hook on the wall near the stove and began to rip it into strips for gags. An urgency to complete what must be done and be gone was pushing at him relentlessly; someone, an old trail acquaintance perhaps, could appear at the door at any moment, dropping by for a drink and to pass the time. If such occurred, he and Red would be forced to fight their way out, for the visitor would certainly sound an alarm before they could stop him.

Tossing half the strips to the redhead, Shawn began to apply those he had to the muttering, cursing outlaws, taking no pains to be gentle, only be thorough. When it was finished, he straightened up and faced Jenny. Wordless, she handed him the sack.

"That all of it?"

She nodded. He glanced about the room, tucked the sack inside his shirt. "Let's get out of here," he said, motioning toward the rear door where Red waited.

Jenny stepped hurriedly over the prone figures of the outlaws. Dolly remained rigid against the wall. Starbuck reached for her.

"No time to waste —"

She drew away. "I'm not going with you — not back there. I've had all of McGraw and that place that I want."

Starbuck swore under his breath. Leaning over, he snatched up a piece of rope. "Suit yourself — I won't force you, but you'll have to be trussed up same as the others."

The woman shook her head. "No, you won't need to. I'll keep quiet — I'll wait until you're gone —"

"The hell she will," Jenny said blandly. "We won't get out of the door before she'll start yelling."

Shawn reached for Dolly's arm and pulled her to the floor with the outlaws. Working swiftly, he secured her wrists and ankles and pulled a strip of the rag tight over her lips. Then, with her burning eyes following him, he crossed to the door where Red and Jenny had paused.

"Let me have a look first," he said.

Drawing in the slab panel carefully, he glanced along the rear of the shacks and Brady's larger building. The area was deserted. Stepping out, he beckoned to Jenny and the redhead and, bent low, led the way at a run to the brush at the lower end of the cleared ground.

The hardpack fronting the structures

89

was also deserted. They hurried on, crossed over and circled around behind the old barn to where the horses waited. At that moment a shout went up from somewhere near the saloon. Shawn wheeled, ran the dozen steps necessary to reach the forward wall of the abandoned stable, and threw his glance to Brady's place.

In the pale flare of the weak lamplight two men had come into the street. Both were staggering from the load of liquor they had consumed, adding to that unsteadiness with periodic gulps from the bottles each held by the neck in his hand. Laughing, shouting, they moved off slowly along the shacks, pointing for those at the lower end.

Starbuck wheeled at once, returned to Red and the girl. Reaching into his shirt, he obtained the sack of money and passed it to the husky rider.

"Take this — her, too," he said, jerking his head at Jenny. "Light out for Babylon."

The redhead jammed the flour sack into a pocket of his saddlebags. Swinging onto the saddle, he reached down, took Jenny's hand, and with Shawn's help, lifted her into place behind him. Only then did he speak.

"What's the trouble?"

"Two drunks — headed for Dallman's maybe. I want you gone if that's what they've got in mind."

"What about you?"

"I aim to be right behind you. If they find Hake and the others and set up a yell, I want to be able to stall them."

"We've got a little spare time. It'll take them a few minutes to get horses."

"I'm counting on that — but you're carrying double . . . I don't want to press things too close."

Red nodded. "Are you going to wait here?"

"No use in that. I'll pull out with you — then drop back so's I can watch."

Shawn turned to his horse, went to the saddle. At once Red spurred away and, with Starbuck close behind, began a wide circle of the camp. They reached the far side with no warning cry rising from the shacks and drew to a halt. Shawn pulled to a small rise from which he could look down at the settlement.

"Expect it'll be smart for me to stall around here for a bit while you go on. If they start to follow, I'll sucker them off into the wrong direction. Just don't think they're going to give up that twenty thousand dollars without a fight."

"No sign of that so far," Red said. "And them two should've reached Dallman's shack by now."

"Looks like we're running in luck," Starbuck admitted, "but I aim to play it safe."

Jenny, silent since they left the shack, shook her head, smiled. "Bart sure knew what he was doing when he hired you. Pity is, you're too dumb to know what it's all about."

Shawn stared at the woman. "There something about my job I don't savvy?"

She shifted on her perch behind Red. "You was hired to be the marshal, sure, but that ain't the big reason he hung that star on you. There's a dozen hanging around the Palace he could have had. But he was looking for somebody special — somebody better'n usual. When he seen you take on Dallman and his bunch, he figured he'd found who he was looking for."

Starbuck, arms folded across his chest, eyes narrowed, waited for Jenny to continue.

"He's not wanting you just to keep things peaceful in the Palace. Your main job is to protect McGraw — he's holed up right now. There's somebody out to kill him, and you've been picked to stand in front of him, keep him alive!"

A faint yell drifted up from Brewer's Flat. Shawn wheeled and threw his glance down the long slope to the collection of shacks. A half a dozen dimly outlined figures were running toward Dallman's house. Without turning, he jerked his head at Red.

"Move out!" he said in a tight voice. "I'll catch up later."

11

Starbuck waited until Red and Jenny had disappeared into the pale night, then, with the girl's words still running through his mind, cut away and rode down the slope to where he had a better view of the camp.

Quite a few men had gathered in the lamplight flare fronting Buffalo Brady's saloon. The distance was too great to be certain, but Starbuck thought he could distinguish Hake Dallman in the crowd; he was not sure, however.

The outlaws milled about and conversed for a time, seemingly undecided as to what course they should follow. Apparently a decision was finally made that pursuit was useless since so much time had elapsed, and the entire group swung about and entered the saloon.

Starbuck shrugged in relief. There would be no trouble for the rest of that night. That Dallman would wait and seek his revenge another time when conditions were more favorable was a foregone conclusion, but that was an emergency best considered when it presented itself.

Wheeling about, Shawn struck for Babylon, Jenny's words still occupying his thoughts and building anger within him with each passing mile.

He rode into the settlement well before dawn. The Palace blazed with lights; that, coupled with a continuing rumble of sound, gave indication that activities were in full swing. Going direct to the stable, he turned the weary sorrel over to a sleepy hostler and headed back to the gambling hall.

His features were set to grim angles as he walked through the doorway. A few shouts of welcome greeted him. He acknowledged them with a slight nod and continued on to the casino area. Halting there, he glanced over the restless crowd, settled his attention finally on one of the dealers standing nearby.

"Where's Fisher?"

The man jerked a thumb at the red door in the rear of the sprawling room. "Office."

Starbuck spun on a heel, crossed to the panel, and entered. Fisher, sitting at a desk, glanced up, frowning at the precipitous entry. His eyes held for a brief time, and then he nodded.

"Glad to see you're back."

Shawn waited out a few moments. When the information he expected was not forthcoming, he said, "Red get here with your money?"

"About an hour ago. What happened to the other girl?"

"She said she didn't want to come back."

The gambler leaned back in his chair. "You could have brought her anyway. We've sunk a lot of money into finding these women and bringing them here. Big investment."

Temper flared through Starbuck. "The hell with your investment! And as far as forcing her was concerned, we didn't have time to argue. I figured it was the money you were most interested in."

Thoughtfully, Bart Fisher drummed on the top of the desk with his finger tips. Finally he shrugged. "Guess it's just as well. Dolly was trouble. Not the first time she'd tried . . . There anything else?"

Starbuck's head bobbed sharply. "Yeh, a little something you forgot to mention when you hired me."

A coldness came into the gambler's eyes. "Go on."

"Jenny tells me my main job around here is to keep your partner alive — that some gunslinger's looking to kill him. That true?"

The gambler studied Shawn for a long minute. "Yes, it is."

Anger flared through Starbuck. "Why the hell didn't you tell me about it at the start?"

"Easy. I was afraid you'd turn down my offer."

"It wouldn't have made any difference," Shawn snapped. "Keeping me in the dark is a good way to get me killed! I haven't been looking for anybody in particular. Do you know who it is?"

Fisher frowned. "You mean this doesn't change anything?"

Starbuck stirred impatiently. "Nothing. Just that it riles me to be led off on a snipe hunt. A man needs to know what he's up against so's he can be ready."

Bart Fisher relaxed gently. "I'm asking your pardon, Starbuck. I'm not used to dealing with your kind, and I'm hoping you'll overlook it and stay with us."

"I'm giving it some thought . . . Where's McGraw? I was told he'd holed up somewhere."

"Jenny tell you that, too?"

"She did."

Fisher's jaw hardened. "It seems she did quite a bit of running off at the mouth . . . It's true. Been hiding out ever since we got word that somebody was coming to kill him. I sent word to him yesterday morning — he's in Dodge — that I had a good man on the job now and that it'd be safe to come back. I expect he'll be here by tonight."

"I asked you before — who's gunning for him?"

"He doesn't know."

"He ought to have some kind of an idea —"

Fisher shrugged. "McGraw's been knocking around for a long time. The Babylon Palace is not the only big gambling house he's ever owned or been connected up with. Expect he's made plenty of enemies — and there'd be a few who'd like to put a bullet in him. Pretty hard for any man to pull himself a step up above the usual crowd without getting somebody sore. Like Dansinger, that gunman you buffaloed your first night on the job."

A fresh wave of anger swept through Starbuck. He was tired, his nerves were raw, and a bitter mood possessed him. "What about it?"

"He sent word by some drifter. Said to

say there wasn't room around here for the both of you — that one of you had to move on."

"Where is he now?"

"At the hotel — staying there."

Shawn wheeled and started for the door. Fisher came up out of his chair.

"That star — you aim to keep wearing it?"

"When I quit, you'll know it," Starbuck snapped, and entering the casino, shouldered his way through the crowd, now beginning to thin with the approach of dawn.

He went directly to the hotel and roused the clerk sleeping on a cot behind the high desk.

"Dansinger — what room's he in?"

The elderly man, not fully awake, stared. "Who?"

"Dansinger!" Shawn repeated irritably. "What's his room number?"

"Four — number four."

Starbuck wheeled and made his way down the faintly lit corridor to the designated door. Drawing his pistol, he gripped the doorknob with his free hand and twisted. It was locked. Temper soaring, he raised his foot and drove in the panel with a crashing kick.

The gunman came off his bed in a quick

bound. He lunged for the gun belt hanging from a nearby chair.

"Touch that and I'll blow you in two!" Starbuck snarled.

Dansinger eased back slowly onto the bed. His features were indistinct in the dim light entering the room through the shade, but he never removed his hard eyes from Starbuck. Out in the hallway there was a faint scraping as the clerk shifted his position, apparently to get a better look at the proceedings.

Shawn drew a match from his pocket, fired it with a thumbnail, and lit the lamp standing on the table. Pulling Dansinger's pistol from its holster, he methodically emptied the cartridges from the cylinder, then dropped it back into place.

"Get your clothes on," he ordered, folding his arms and leaning against the wall. "You're pulling out."

The gunman stared at him coldly for a long breath and then began to dress. Finished, he reached cautiously for his belt.

"Hang it on your shoulder," Starbuck said quietly.

Dansinger complied wordlessly. Shawn jerked his head at the door. "Let's go . . . I'm walking you to the stable."

The gunman turned at once, moved out

into the hall, and, with Starbuck a stride behind him, entered the lobby, passed by the gaping clerk, and stepped into the street, now bright with the first rosy flare of the new day.

The same drowsy hostler brought Dansinger's horse, threw the gear into place, and aware of the brittle tension lying between the two men, hurriedly moved away. The gunslinger swung onto the saddle, cut his horse around, and started for the wide entrance. He drew rein, then twisted about to face Shawn.

"This ain't the last verse. Reckon you know that."

"I know . . . Your kind never learns until it's too late."

"Nobody rousts me and lives to brag about it. I'll be looking to square up."

Shawn's wide shoulders stirred. "Take my advice, forget it. You maybe'll get me — but I'll kill you doing it."

Dansinger nodded slowly as if considering the truth of the statement. "Could be," he murmured, and rode on, turning south as he came onto the hardpack.

Starbuck, the anger and frustration that had gripped him since he had walked in to face Bart Fisher earlier that morning finally diminishing, watched the gunman move off . . . Another customer for Buffalo Brady. Like as not he would join Hake Dallman's crowd. Shawn smiled grimly. The number of hopefuls seeking to put a bullet in his hide was growing.

12

Starbuck slept until late afternoon. Rising, he treated himself to a shave and scrubbing in the tin tub provided for such; after which, feeling much better, he drew on clean clothing and went into the street.

His belly was again clamoring for food. When Dansinger had ridden off, discredited and beaten to the punch by the very man he had challenged, Shawn had gone on to his quarters and retired, all inclination to partake of a morning meal lost in the splintery tension that had gripped him. Now that it was all behind him, hunger once more was an issue.

Moving by the Palace, he nodded to several men standing at the hitchrack, gave no thought to their cool, remote response, and made his way to the restaurant.

Bessie, a large blonde somewhere in her late forties, met him inside the doorway. Like the girls at the Palace she, too, went in heavily for cosmetics, and Shawn had wondered before if she at some previous time had not followed a similar occupation. That she had been a handsome, if not actually a beautiful woman was apparent; but the years had exacted their toll, withering the fairness, leaving only a grossness of sagging skin and harsh lines.

"Your friend's waiting," she said, and pointed a thick finger at Red sitting near a window.

Shawn crossed to the husky rider and smiled his greeting.

The redhead yawned, stretched. "I'm glad to see you ain't packing no lead," he said as Starbuck drew up a chair. "I've been wondering what happened after me and the woman left, but I didn't want to wake you."

"Nothing," Shawn answered. "Looked like they had the notion for a bit to start chasing us, then gave it up."

Red shrugged. "Not for long — you can bet on that."

"For sure — and they'll have a new gun to take the Kid's place."

"That jasper you run out of town this morning?"

"The same . . . How'd you know about it? Wasn't anybody around."

"Well, everybody knows about it now. The hotel clerk and the hostler down at the barn — they spread the story fast."

Starbuck nodded slowly. That accounted for the attitude of the men he had passed at the rack. He was now one apart, a dangerous man best left alone. He had had a taste of it that first night; his encounter with Dansinger further isolated him. . . . It didn't matter — was better that way, in fact.

"What're you having?" Bessie asked, halting beside the table. "Reckon Bart'll want you to have the best in the house after what you done."

"Count Red here on that, too," Starbuck replied. "He was there."

The buxom woman's thick shoulders stirred. "Sure. I'll fix you both up good," she said, and turned away for the kitchen.

Shawn felt the redhead's eyes upon him. He grinned. "Don't you go giving me the cold stare now! Not expecting it from my friends."

"You might as well get used to it — but I was thinking about something else, about what Jenny said."

"McGraw? I jumped Fisher when I rode in. It's true. Somebody is out to put a slug

105

in him, and they're looking to me to stop it."

"They know who?"

Shawn wagged his head and stared off onto the hardpack. The men at the hitchrack had mounted, were swinging onto the east road that led to Wichita and neighboring points.

"Fisher only said McGraw had enemies, plenty of them, who'd like to cut him down if they got the chance. Couldn't tell me much else."

Red took a sip of his coffee. It was cold. He returned the cup to its saucer, pushed it away.

"I sort of like working in the dark."

"That's what it amounts to."

"You aim to stay on the job?"

"Reckon so. I was mighty hot and close to quitting when I collared Fisher about it; then I simmered down. I can't see as it'll be any different from handling somebody like Dansinger. Just have to watch sharper."

Bessie appeared, bringing a pot of fresh coffee. She filled Shawn's cup, dumped what was left in Red's into a nearby cuspidor, and poured him another portion.

"Heard McGraw'd be coming back now," the redhead said. "Guess they figure it's safe."

"Due in tonight, so Fisher thinks. He's been holed up in Dodge."

"If I ain't wrong," Bessie said mildly, "that'll be the old tub-of-guts now."

Shawn gave the heavy woman a quizzical look and swung his attention to the cleared area. A buggy containing two passengers was rolling up to the stable next to the Palace. It came to a halt, and a thickset man, well dressed in a gray suit, polished Hyer boots, and a flat-crowned white hat, stepped down.

A hostler appeared magically, caught at the bridle of the off horse to steady the team as McGraw moved to assist his companion, a young and pretty girl.

"What I figured — he's gone and picked himself a new one," Bessie muttered in a low voice.

Starbuck glanced again at the elderly woman, conscious of the bitterness that tinged her words. Evidently there had been a time when she and Amos McGraw had been close — a period when she had been the favored one — only to be shunted aside for another.

"Quite a looker," he said without thinking.

"Always are," Bessie snapped. "But she won't last long. Too much of a kid."

"He ever bring in any other kind but kids?" Red asked dryly.

The portly McGraw, offering his crooked arm to the girl, stepped away from the buggy. Together they moved toward the Palace, he gesturing at its ornate façade and speaking volubly as they drew nearer. Her round face was tipped up. She was smiling, and her eyes were wide with wonder as she listened in rapt silence.

"How's that star you're wearing feel on you now, Marshal?" the redhead asked, his tone faintly sardonic.

Shawn watched McGraw and the girl cross the Palace gallery at a leisurely step and disappear into its interior. He shifted on his chair.

"No different. What he does is his business. I draw my pay for keeping the peace around here. Seeing that he stays alive is a part of it."

"It don't bother you that he talks, maybe even forces those girls into coming here so's he can rent them out — make a part of his living off them?"

"I would if I thought they were being forced. She sure wasn't — she knows what it's all about, and that part of him's no concern of mine. I just have to keep him from getting filled with lead —"

"Which he ain't worth!" Bessie cut in flatly. "Was you smart, you'd move on, find yourself a good woman, marry her, and settle down. Hanging around trash like Amos McGraw and Bart Fisher ain't for you! I can see that in your eyes."

"A job's a job —"

"This one ain't. You'd be doing the country a big favor was you to let whoever it is after him, kill him!"

Starbuck grinned. "You're a bloodthirsty old woman, Bessie," he said. "How about that grub? I'm flat-out starved."

The woman's lips clamped shut, and whirling, she hurried off.

"Don't think she likes McGraw much," the redhead drawled. "Ain't you trotting over to shake his hand?"

"No hurry," Shawn replied, leaning back as Bessie reappeared almost immediately, bringing a platter of food in each hand.

She placed the dishes before them in silence and moved away, evidently having said all she intended to say on the matter. Starbuck began to eat at once, finding the thick steak and gravy-smothered mashed potatoes exactly to his liking.

The two men finished their meal, one topped off with hot apple pie and more coffee, and then rose to leave. Red paid his check over Shawn's protest, and both moved out into the darkening street.

"Reckon I'll see you later," the husky redhead said, angling for the hotel's entrance. "After a pile of eats like that, I need a nap."

Starbuck nodded. It was early for making his rounds of the stores, but he felt an urge to walk and settle such a fine supper before taking up a stand inside the gambling hall.

"I'll be looking for you," he said, and stepping off the landing, he cut right, crossed in front of the barber shop and its adjacent neighbor where guns and saddles were sold, repaired, and often pawned and trail supplies could be had.

Rounding the corner of the low-roofed structure, he continued on, walking slowly, enjoying the cool breeze that had sprung into being . . . He had not let working for men like McGraw and Bart Fisher worry him; his primary purpose there was to find out what, if anything, could be learned of Ben, and as he had been told, there was no better place than Babylon to accomplish that.

He gained the end of the saddle shop, turned the corner into the alley that ran behind the structures, and halted. On to the west a short distance, where the cottonwoods and elms and dogwood stood thick along the creek, a dove was mourning into the coming night, the call plaintive and lonely in the hush.

It was an evening that took him swiftly back over the years to Muskingum, to the farm where Ben and he had spent their growing years — the same quiet of late summer, the sweet smells of grass and clover, the light clean blue of the sky turning to velvet as the sun's burnished flare softened and faded.

Life had been good, pleasant. Their mother, tall and coolly efficient, would have been preparing supper; their father, his labors of the day finished, would be in the big cowhide-and-oak chair placed under the sycamore that spread its thickly leafed branches over the house. He would be smoking his curved-stem pipe, eyes thoughtful as he stared out over the land he loved so deeply.

He and Ben would be finishing their chores, or if they had already completed their assigned tasks, they would be playing at mumblety-peg on the bench near the pump house or perhaps scuffling about in the soft mat at the foot of the haystack.

Over all would be hanging the faint,

amber haze that comes with late summer, but a noticeable sharpness would be tinge- ing the breeze as if reminding them all that winter was not far off and that soon the snows and cutting winds would lay a still- ness upon it all.

It had been a happy life, one that saw the beginning of the end when Clare Starbuck died, a victim of lung fever, one further hastened by Ben's stormy departure two years later and that came to a final, irrevo- cable finish eight years later when old Hiram passed to whatever reward or pun- ishment his Maker had in store for him.

The completion of one lifetime, the begin- ning of another, that is what the death of the elder Starbuck had meant to Shawn — the finale of one phase, the rising curtain to an- other. But he had adapted, as he knew he must, embracing the new, hostile, grimly harsh style of existence with a calm resolu- tion that would have made Clare and Hiram proud of him. He had set his mind —

"Marshal, don't turn around — please!"

At the sound of the cautious words, Starbuck stiffened. It was a woman's voice coming from the side of the building he had just moved past.

"Who're you?" he asked, keeping his eyes straight ahead.

"Somebody you don't know. I'd like to keep it that way."

It would be one of the girls from the Palace, he realized. "What's this all about?"

"Something you ought to know —"

"About what?"

"A friend of yours. Go to room number eleven in the hotel . . . See for yourself."

13

The guarded words were followed by the quiet rustle of cloth, then silence. Shawn turned about. There was no one in sight.

He considered what he had heard . . . Room eleven . . . A friend of his. He thought back, tried to recall the voice, failed; he sought then to determine who the friend might be. He had actually made few so far during his short time in Babylon — Red, the bartender, Pete, and, of course, Bart Fisher. It could be a trap of some sort, but who would be at the bottom of it? Dallman and his crowd were not around; neither was the gunman, Dansinger.

There was but one way to find out. He started for the street, hesitated. To enter the hotel by its front door meant drawing the attention of the clerk, and after his experience with Dansinger, he would as soon avoid that. Wheeling, he cut back down the alley to the rear of the building and let himself in through that entrance.

The hallway was dark, a solitary lamp burning at its far end, just off the lobby, the only source of light; stepping up to the nearest door, he checked the number. It was twelve. He swung about to the one on the opposite side of the corridor . . . eleven.

Drawing his pistol, he moved in close and placed his ear against the panel. There was no sound. Reaching for the knob, he turned it carefully. There was a dry click, but the door failed to yield . . . Locked. He heard a moan then as if he had aroused whoever was inside.

Holstering his weapon, he slid his fingers into his left boot and procured the slim-bladed knife he carried. Forcing its point between the edge of the door's frame and the lock housing, he pried. The tumbler gave, and the panel swung inward, releasing a gust of hot stale air.

Shawn waited there, allowing his eyes to adjust to the deeper darkness. The shades were drawn, and he could make out little other than that there was a shape lying on the bed.

"Who — who is it?" The voice was low, exhausted, and unmistakably Jenny's.

Shawn stepped into the room quickly

and closed the door. Thumbnailing a match into life, he crossed to the table beside the bed and lit the lamp that stood upon it.

Jenny, battered almost beyond recognition, stared up at him from pain-filled eyes that were all but buried in a swollen, discolored face. Her dress was in shreds, and the portions of her body visible through the tears were covered by dark welts. She lay flat, unmoving, as if to stir was painful beyond bearing.

A gust of anger rocked Starbuck. "Who did this to you?"

Jenny's crushed lips scarcely moved. "Fisher —"

"Fisher. Why?"

"Because — I — I talked — told you about — McGraw."

Shawn, pity tempering the wild anger that had gripped him at first sight of the gambler's sadistic handiwork, sat down on the edge of the bed, doing it slowly, carefully so as to not cause the girl more pain.

"I wish't now I'd done like Dolly — not come back."

"If you don't want to stay, you won't have to," Starbuck said gently.

Jenny sighed heavily. "You — you don't

know how it is. They won't let me — leave."

"If you want to go, I'll see to it. The doctor been here yet?"

"No —"

"Why not? How long have you been here?"

"Since — this morning. The doctor — he's afraid to come."

"He'll come," Starbuck said flatly. "Where'll I find him?"

"The barber shop — in the back. But there's no need. Not much — he can do that Hallie — a friend ain't already done."

Hallie would be the woman who had spoken to him in the alley. She evidently had come to Jenny's aid at great risk to herself.

"Best he see you anyway. He can give you something to ease the pain."

"No — it'll mean trouble for you — with Bart."

"I can handle it," Starbuck said, rising. "I'll be right back."

Leaving the room, he entered the hall and returned to the alley. The barber shop was immediately to his left. Moving to it, he tried the doorknob. It was locked; doubling his fist, he rapped sharply. After a moment the panel opened and a tall, hawk-faced man peered out at him.

"I'm looking for the doctor."

The man half turned, took up a lamp that was nearby, and held it above his head for better light. He nodded briskly.

"Oh, it's you, Marshal. I'm Gilman — what's the trouble?"

"Friend of mine. Like for you to come."

"Sure," the medical man said, setting the lamp down and reaching for his coat.

"Won't need that," Shawn said. "Only going next door."

The doctor released the garment and picked up a leather satchel bearing faded, gold-lettered words, *J. Gilman . . . M.D.*, on its side.

"The hotel? Never heard anything —"

Ignoring the man's doubt, Starbuck held the door open and hurried him out into the alley and on into the rear entrance of the hostelry. Gilman paused there, waited while Shawn moved ahead of him to the room in which Jenny had been placed.

The medical man entered, halted abruptly when his eyes settled upon the woman. Half turning, he shook his head. "Now wait a minute — I can't interfere —"

Starbuck had closed the door and was standing against it, pistol in hand.

"If you expect to walk out of here, you'll

do what you can for her," he said coldly.

Gilman frowned, wiped at the sweat suddenly glistening on his narrow face. "But Fisher — McGraw — if I —"

"They won't do anything about it if you tell them I held a gun on you. No need for them to know, anyway, far as I can see."

"It's all right," Jenny murmured weakly. "I don't want to make more trouble for —"

"Get at it, Doc," Starbuck cut in. "I damn well meant what I said!"

Gilman shrugged and crossed to the bed. Moving the lamp closer, he examined the woman carefully, pressing, probing, moving her arms and legs, turning her head gently from side to side, peering into her mouth, eyes, and ears. When he was finished, he looked up.

"A bad beating, nothing more. No broken bones. Teeth all intact . . . Not much I can do except give her something to make her sleep."

"You sure that's all?"

The medical man, digging about in his satchel, paused, fixed his eyes on Starbuck. "That's all," he said quietly. "Was there anything else, I'd be obliged to do it . . . Besides, I learned a long time ago that it was stupid to argue with a man holding a gun."

Shawn dropped his weapon back into its holster, and pulled away from the door. Gilman concluded his ministrations, snapped the bag shut, and turned.

Starbuck said, "I'm obliged to you. Nobody else needs to know about your coming here. It won't be mentioned unless it's by you."

Gilman smiled faintly. "One thing I never do is discuss my patients," he said, and opening the door, disappeared into the dark hallway.

Shawn crossed to where Jenny lay and looked down at her. The tautness of pain was fading from her bruised features and the brightness that had filled her eyes was dulling.

"Thank . . . you," she murmured.

"It's all right. Just stay quiet and rest. Nobody will bother you, and soon as you're able to travel, I'll see about getting you out of town."

She roused slightly. "You — you can do that?"

"Sure. Any place special you'd like to go?"

"Wichita . . . I have some friends there."

"Then Wichita it is. How about something to eat?"

"I'm not hungry."

"You will be when you wake up. I'll talk to Bessie, get her to bring you something . . . Fisher and McGraw don't scare her any."

Jenny managed a wan smile. "No — they sure don't . . . Thank you, again. Can you stay — a while?"

Her words dragged. The sedative Gilman had given her was beginning to take effect.

"Sure, but it's time I moved on, let you rest. I'll drop by later when I make my rounds."

He could have saved his breath. Jenny was asleep. Setting the lamp farther back on the table, he turned it low and left the room. Again using the rear door, he left the hotel, circled the building, and came around to the restaurant.

Bessie was in conversation with the woman cook as he entered; calling her aside, Starbuck explained the situation in a few quick words.

The corners of Bessie's mouth pulled down. Her thick shoulders stirred with disinterest. "Let one of them other sluts look after her . . . she got what she had coming."

Starbuck, surprised, stared at the older woman's sagging features. "She didn't deserve that," he snapped. "And far as one of the others helping her — they won't. They're all afraid."

Again Bessie shrugged. "That supposed to make me bleed?"

The bitterness in her tone did not escape Shawn. There was an intensity of feeling that went deeper than envy — jealousy, perhaps, and a strong hatred. He gave that thought, then switched his approach.

"Aim to get her out of here soon as she can travel," he said. "Wants to go to Wichita. I'm going to see that she makes it."

Bessie's expression did not change.

"I know how you feel about McGraw and Fisher. Helping me help her is one way you can spite the both of them."

The woman's eyes flickered. "How you going to get her out of here?"

"I'll manage."

"They'll stop you. They won't let any of them go until they ain't of no more use."

"That's going to change. Jenny'll be on her way to Wichita quick as she can make the trip. Any of the others wants to go along, they'll be welcome."

"What about McGraw — and Bart Fisher?"

"I'll take care of that part of it. You willing to help?"

Bessie hesitated for a long moment, then bobbed her head. "I'll do what I can," she said. "What room's Jenny in?"

"Number eleven," Starbuck replied, and turning back to the street, pointed for the Babylon Palace. Bart Fisher was due a dose of his own medicine.

14

Grim, a sullen determination bordering on keen anticipation gripping him as he thought of giving the gambler the same merciless kind of beating that had been administered Jenny, Shawn stepped up onto the gallery fronting the Babylon Palace.

He paused, arrested by the singular hush that lay over the place. At that hour the Palace ordinarily would be throbbing with activity and noise. Instead, it was as if the place were deserted.

Frowning, his wrath toward Bart Fisher momentarily fading into the background of his mind, Starbuck pressed forward quietly. Hand resting on the butt of his pistol, he passed through the wide doorway into the lamplight-flooded saloon.

The stilled crowd had drawn back against the walls. Eyes upon two poised drovers, their faces were taut, expectant as they awaited that fragment of time when hands would go flashing down for pistols and the room would rock with the explosions that would mean death for one, possibly both.

Intervention at such a moment could ordinarily be a mistake. An argument, progressed to the point of challenge and showdown, should be permitted to run to its conclusion; any man attempting to halt those natural proceedings was taking a long chance.

But the casino was packed, and the danger from stray bullets was far too great to ignore.

Walking softly, Starbuck crossed to the center of the area and angled toward the pair, approaching them from the side and on a course that would take him into the exact middle of the space that separated them. In so doing he was giving each man equal opportunity to become aware of his presence.

Shawn was a fraction late. He drew his pistol and started to call out to the pair, to caution them not to make a move for their weapons. As the first word formed on his lips, the drover to his right buckled slightly. The man facing him took a half step left. In that identical instant the crash of two heavy weapons blasted the quiet within the

Palace into a bedlam of rocking echoes.

A yell of pain went up from a man standing with several others among the poker tables as a deflected bullet smashed into his leg. The drover to Shawn's right leaned forward on his toes, wavered uncertainly, and fell, his weapon, released from nerveless fingers, striking the floor with a thud and skittering off to one side.

Immediately Starbuck crossed through the layers of drifting, acrid smoke to the other rider. The man hung motionless, the barrel of his pistol tipped down as he stared at his lifeless opponent.

"I'll take that," Shawn said harshly, and wrenched the weapon from his grasp. "You're under arrest."

As if coming from a deep slumber, the drover roused slowly and turned his eyes on Starbuck. "What?"

"You're coming to jail," Shawn replied, and as the crowd, paralysis broken, surged forward, he lifted his hand in warning. "Stay back! A couple of you carry the dead man outside — see about burying him. The rest of you go on about your business."

"I'm hit — shot —"

Starbuck swung his attention to the wounded bystander. He jerked his head at those standing near. "Get him over to Doc Gilman's," he ordered, and once again came back to the gunman. "Let's go, mister."

The drover frowned, did not move. "Was a fair shoot-out —"

"Maybe, but you picked the wrong place to hold it."

Taking the man by the arm, he pulled him about and, ignoring the mutter of protests that instantly arose from obvious friends, marched him toward the door. Reaching that point, Shawn looked back. The drover's friends had threatened, but they were not acting; satisfied, he pushed his grumbling prisoner through the door- way and continued on to the jail where he locked him in one of the cells.

Once again in the street he paused. Several men were now standing in front of the barber shop; and he guessed the luckless customer accidentally shot in the altercation was receiving Gilman's attention. The dead man, he supposed, had been taken there, too, as usually the town physician also served as coroner and quite often as undertaker.

The tenseness within him began to fade, and the deep anger accompanying his original purpose, shunted to the side when the emergency arose, lifted to the surface again. At once he struck off along the street, moving in an erect, purposeful manner toward the Palace. Entering, he found all things back to normalcy, plainly uninhibited to any extent whatever by the death of one man, the wounding of another.

Nodding brusquely to the half a dozen or so persons who sought to compliment him on his actions, he pushed through the crowd to where Bart Fisher was holding forth at a roulette wheel.

"Got something to take up with you," he said in a low, uncompromising voice.

The gambler's brows raised slightly at the tone. He half turned, beckoned to one of the dealers, and then wheeling, led the way to the office at the rear of the casino.

As they entered, Amos McGraw, seated at the desk going through a sheaf of papers, looked up. He had small, hard-surfaced eyes that stared out from a flaccid, joweled face with unblinking constancy. There was an oiliness to him and instantaneous dislike stirred through Starbuck.

Fisher halted, motioned at Shawn. "Amos, this is our new marshal — one I told you about. You just saw how he works."

McGraw's fishlike gaze did not change. "I like the way you're doing things," he said.

Starbuck folded his arms across his chest. He shook his head. "I don't like the way you are."

The older man eased back into his chair slowly. Bart Fisher's mouth tightened. "That what you came here to say?"

"It is."

"Then say it."

"I'm talking about Jenny — what you did to her. I aim to give you a little of the same treatment."

A half smile pulled at the gambler's lips. He reached into an inside pocket of his coat and drew out a cigar. Biting off its end, he probed for a match.

"Wouldn't be very smart, Marshal," he murmured.

Amos McGraw brushed at the sweat beading his forehead with an impatient swipe of his thick hand. "What the hell's this all about?"

"Jenny," Fisher said, lighting his match and puffing the cigar into life, "was shooting off her mouth. I had to teach her a lesson."

McGraw shrugged, shifted his weight. "So? What's wrong with that?"

"Plenty!" Starbuck snapped, temper rising within him. "There was no need for it. She did nothing wrong except tell me a few things I should have been told in the first place."

"I don't deny that — and I apologized," Fisher said, exhaling a cloud of smoke. "But it wasn't her place to go spouting off."

"And there was no call for you to beat her half to death either!"

McGraw laced his fingers together, considered Shawn coldly. "Now, hold on, Marshal, I don't figure that's any of your business," he said.

There was a trace of accent to his words, the faintly rounded edges of the South. Starbuck's jaw hardened. "Happens I'm making it my business."

"Don't," McGraw continued. "But so's you'll know the why of it, women of her stripe have to be handled like that. Have to be held in check, made to remember they're here for only one thing, and that anything they see or hear ain't to be carried on."

"Exactly," Fisher declared. "It's necessary to work them over now and then.

Only way we can keep them in line."

"Not the way I see it," Starbuck said. "No woman deserves that kind of roughing up —"

"You're wrong, boy," McGraw broke in, a forced smile splitting his mouth. "You don't know nothing about whores, and we do. Best thing you can do is forget coming in here and spouting off. You leave them to us and take care of your own job . . . You're doing fine at it. I was just thinking about talking to Bart, seeing if we couldn't up your wages a notch or two."

"Forget it — I'm not interested. And far as your job's concerned, you can —"

"Now, don't do something rash!" McGraw cut in, stirred to haste for the first time. "This here's all unnecessary. Maybe Bart did go a mite far punishing the girl, but I reckon he felt it was needful . . . That right, Bart?"

Fisher's shoulders lifted, fell. "Could be, but you never know how much is enough when you're dealing with her kind. They're hard — tough. Takes a plenty to make them remember." The gambler paused, took a deep draft of his cigar, and exhaled. "How'd you find out about her, Marshal?"

Shawn favored the gambler with a humorless grin. "Was a little bird . . . Now, soon as she's able, she'll be leaving here. I'm arranging it — and if anything happens to her in the meantime, you'll both answer to me."

McGraw and his partner exchanged glances. The older man cocked his head to one side and studied Shawn. "You figure to make her your woman, that it?"

"No, feel the same if it had been one of the others — or if it was some man who couldn't take care of himself."

"I see . . . This your price for staying on the job?"

"That's it, and I don't much care which way it goes."

"Well, we're agreeing . . . Now, how about talking a bit about the main reason you were hired for — looking out for me. You got any special plan in mind to trap him?"

Starbuck shrugged. "Not much I can do but keep watch over you when you're out in the open."

"About all you can do," McGraw said; and casting a sly glance at Fisher, he added, "Don't expect to be out and around much for the next few days. Got something that's going to keep me plenty busy. You might —"

A quick knock sounded on the door. It

opened immediately to admit Pete. The barman, one hand on the knob, the other braced against the frame, leaned in.

"Marshal — thought you better know. Them Texan friends of Gannon's are aiming to bust him out of jail!"

15

Starbuck spun on a heel. He checked himself as Amos McGraw's exasperated voice caught him.

"My God — you didn't jail that man did you?"

"Of course I did!" Shawn snapped. "He killed —"

"I know that, but all you should've done was take him outside, send him on his way."

"What kind of law and order is that? Can't expect to keep it if I'm to stand by and let any cowhand with a chip on his shoulder settle his differences with a gun inside the place. Too many people could get hurt."

"He's right, Amos," Fisher said. "One customer did get winged by a stray bullet, and it could have been worse. Be smart to get word spread around that we'll stand for no gun play inside the place."

"Far as I'm concerned, it's already stopped," Starbuck said. "Starting tomorrow every man coming in will have to check his gun at the door. I'll talk to you about that later."

He waited no longer, but moved hurriedly into the saloon, cut through the crowd that appeared either unaware or uninterested in the assault of the jail planned by Gannon's friends, and passed through the doorway.

Reaching the street, Starbuck threw his glance toward the end of the building. The Texans had halted in front of the feed store and were tearing a packing crate to bits for torches.

Moving fast, he ducked into the livery stable, ran its length to the rear, and entering the alley, circled the structure to reach his own quarters. Walking through them, he came into the jail just as Gannon's friends crowded up to the entrance. Snatching a shotgun from the rack, Shawn stepped forward to block them.

"Back off!" he yelled, leveling the weapon.

The dozen or so men hesitated, fell back a step, the flaming torches held above their heads flickering brightly, lending a ruddy glow to their angry faces.

"We're wanting Tom Gannon, Marshal
. . . Turn him loose!" a voice cried.

"I'm not about to," Starbuck replied
evenly.

"What the hell you jug him for?" another
demanded. "Man's got a right to stand and
draw."

"He can do it anytime he likes as long as
he's out in the open where nobody else'll
get hurt."

"Is it murder you're holding him for?"

"Disturbing the peace . . . Move on — or
you'll all be in there locked up with him."

"Just you try locking —"

The crowd parted. Amos McGraw, sided
by Fisher, moved briskly up to the landing,
halted just outside the doorway.

"It's all right, boys," McGraw said,
facing the muttering, threatening punchers. "No need for this . . . The marshal's
only doing his job."

"Maybe — but we ain't letting him keep
Tom —"

"He won't," McGraw answered, holding
both hands aloft for silence. "I'm judge
here in Babylon. I'll straighten things out
for you."

Starbuck, lowering his shotgun, turned
angrily to the older man. "You want things
kept under control around here, you claim.

Interfering's not going to make it —"

"I'm not interfering," McGraw responded smoothly. "Just speeding up justice a bit, holding trial now. What's the charge?"

"Disturbing the peace —"

McGraw looked out over the Texans. "Charge against your friend Gannon is for disturbing the peace. I'm naming you the jury. Is he guilty?"

There was no immediate answer. McGraw waited a long minute, then said, "Is there any doubt in your minds that he fired off a pistol inside the Babylon Palace?"

"No, reckon not," a rider in the front of the crowd said. "But you can't —"

"Then he is guilty as charged. It's my duty to fine him twenty-five dollars —"

A howl of disagreement went up. McGraw again raised his hands, palms out, for silence. Bart Fisher stepped up onto the landing. Reaching into a pocket, he produced a roll of currency. Peeling off several of the bills, he passed them to Shawn.

"Here you are, Marshal — money for Gannon's fine. Now you can turn him loose."

Another shout echoed into the night.

Starbuck stared at the money, baffled, for a brief time; then, wheeling, he turned back into his office. Dropping the bills on his desk, he stood the shotgun against the rack and, taking the keys, unlocked the cell and permitted the grinning Gannon to step out.

"My iron," the puncher said, halting in the center of the room.

Shawn jerked open a drawer, recovered the Texan's pistol, and handed it to him.

"Keep it in the leather, long as you're around here," he warned quietly.

Tom Gannon's grin widened. "Sure will, Marshal," he said, and swaggered out to join his friends.

Starbuck followed the man to the doorway. The Texans broke into cheers at once, some rushing forward to claim their member and pound him on the back. A little to one side of the milling men, Shawn caught sight of Red. The husky rider, arms crossed upon his chest, was watching it all with a look of dry amusement on his features.

"You satisfied, Marshal?"

At Amos McGraw's question, Starbuck came about. The two owners of the settlement were standing beside his desk.

"Everything's all settled — and no harm done."

"Doesn't make much sense —"

"Does to us," the older man said flatly. "We don't want anybody, especially the trail hands, going away sore. Business depends on them and their coming back to Babylon every chance they get. Paying Gannon's fine makes everybody happy — them, you, and us."

"Nobody loses," Bart Fisher added.

Shawn admitted silently that such was fact. No one was out anything since the money collected as a fine went back into the pockets of McGraw and Fisher — but insofar as the law was concerned, it was a mockery.

"Maybe so, but you might as well not have a marshal. Idea will get around fast that a man can get away with anything here as long as he's a big spender."

"I suppose so — eventually," McGraw murmured, wiping at the sweat on his face. "But you've got to bear in mind that Babylon is a place where trail hands — along with anybody else — can blow off steam. We're willing to take our chances on how they do it, long as they blow their cash here, too."

"This the way you've been doing it all along?"

"Mostly. Been a few times when we let

139

the prisoner pay off himself. Try to avoid that, however, when it's a bunch like those Texans. They're usually pretty wild and don't much give a damn what they do."

"In other words it's all according to who it is. If the man's not apt to fight back or doesn't have a bunch of friends with him, you take his money. If it's somebody like Gannon, you pay off for him yourself."

"About the size of it," McGraw drawled. "And we're still in business and going strong."

Starbuck looked down at the star pinned to his shirt. Little by little it was becoming less meaningful. To him the law was a living fact, a trust to be maintained and not circumvented. He shook his head slowly.

"I don't know about this. Maybe —"

"I've been thinking about something you said," McGraw went on. "I was talking it over with Bart."

"About making customers check their guns when they come into the Palace," Fisher added, noting Shawn's frown. "We think you've got a smart idea."

"I figure we could set up a rack just inside the door," the older man said. "We'd keep somebody standing right there, maybe a deputy, to look after it."

"I thought we'd nail up a sign outside saying that anybody entering had to check his weapon," Bart Fisher continued. "That ought to eliminate a lot of argument."

"It works in Dodge City," Starbuck said. "Should here, too."

"No doubt will, especially if you're standing around to see that it's done — friendly like, of course."

"Of course," Shawn repeated dryly. "We don't want to rile anybody."

"Exactly. I can't see as it'll cause any problems. A man knowing every other man in the place is unarmed won't buck at checking his gun."

"I was thinking, too," Fisher said, staring off through the doorway at Gannon and his friends, now mounting their horses at the rack preparatory to riding on, "be one way of stopping whoever this fellow is who's supposed to be coming after Amos —"

"Supposed to be!" McGraw snapped. "No doubt in my mind about it!"

"None in mine, either," the gambler said hastily.

"I didn't mean that the way it sounded. Anyway, making everybody coming into the Palace hand over his pistol ought to make it easier for you to spot him."

"How?" Shawn wondered.

"Anybody refusing to obey the rule will bear watching."

"Unless McGraw's outside — in the open."

"I never do much of that," the older man said.

"You came here —"

"Could say this was an emergency. It won't happen again — leastwise I'm hoping you won't let it," McGraw added pointedly.

Starbuck made no answer, only shrugged.

"Anyway, the plan's bound to help. We'll put it in effect tomorrow."

Abruptly McGraw turned for the door and, followed by Bart Fisher, moved out into the street. Shawn stepped to the opening, halted. The Texans were pulling away, all laughing noisily and shouting back and forth. As the owners of the Palace drew abreast, they raised their hands and yelled something that drew cheers from the drovers as they spurred off.

Starbuck watched McGraw and Fisher gain the porch of the gambling house, then cross and disappear into its brightly lit interior. Coming back around, his eyes fell upon the money laying on his desk. Fisher had neglected to reclaim it.

Stuffing it into his shirt pocket, he turned down the lamps and started for the door. He would take it to the gambler, spend a few more hours in the Palace, and then make his rounds of the business houses — sparing time to drop by and visit Jenny and to tell her that she was free to depart whenever she felt physically able. After that he was turning in — not so much because he was tired. It was simply that he wanted to be alone to do some serious thinking about this job as the marshal of Babylon.

16

There were three patrons in the café that next morning when Shawn, after a somewhat restless night, entered. All were cowhands en route to some distant point, up early in the interests of getting a good start. As Starbuck moved across the room to his customary table near the window, he nodded to them. They responded coolly.

The hell with all of you, he thought, and settled down. Bessie emerged from the rear of the establishment bringing coffee and setting it before him. "You waiting for your friend?"

"No, expect he'll be along shortly," Shawn replied. "Bring me the usual."

"Jenny's doing fine," the older woman said grudgingly.

"I know that. I saw her last night. Obliged to you."

Bessie's thick shoulders moved. "Ain't nothing," she said, and headed back for the kitchen. A solitary rider came in on the east road, paused to stare at the Babylon Palace, and then swung into the livery stable. Somewhere back of all the buildings a dog barked nervously. The three punchers arose, dropped coins on the table for their meal, and stamped out heavily, looking neither right nor left as they walked toward the hitchrack.

Bessie reentered the room and crossed to him with his order of bacon and eggs. Placing it before him, she pulled back a chair opposite, sat down, her overripe features drawn into a frown.

Shawn gave her a close look. "Something wrong?"

"I've been thinking about Jenny."

He paused, a forkful of meat and eggs halfway to his mouth. "What about her?"

"She's planning strong on leaving here."

Starbuck nodded. "I told her she could when she was ready."

"You for sure meaning it?"

"Hell, yes, I mean it!" he replied impatiently, hesitating again.

The woman shifted her bulk. "What about McGraw?"

"I already told him. Be no problem."

"That's sure mighty funny. He ain't never let one of them go before unless he figured they wasn't no good to him no more . . . Then he run them off himself."

"It could be that's all going to change."

Shawn felt that woman's eyes drilling into him. After a moment she said, "There some reason you're doing this for Jenny — some private reason, I mean — like maybe you're wanting her for yourself?"

"No, just lending a hand."

A long sigh slipped from Bessie's lips. "Jesus," she murmured, "I guess I plumb forgot there was still folks like you around . . . Just helping her . . . Hard to believe."

"That's the way it is. Figuring how to do it is the next thing. Not being any stage-coach running through here makes it a problem. She wants to go to Wichita."

"That was what she told me. Best thing's for her to go to Dodge first. Be easy from there on."

Starbuck nodded. "Heard of anybody making the trip?"

"Only drovers and cowhands — all riding horseback. Not many around here ever use a buggy except McGraw."

"I doubt if she's in shape to fork a horse that far. Got to find some other way."

Bessie pursed her lips. "How about your friend Red? Maybe you could talk him into driving her. Kiefer at the stable's got a buggy he rents out now and then."

Shawn's head came up. "That's the answer! Red's just loafing around. I'm pretty sure he'll be willing to do it. When'll Jenny be able to leave?"

"Better give her a couple more days. That Fisher beat her something fierce. The back side of her is nigh solid black from all the kicking he done."

"I had a little talk with him and McGraw both about that," Starbuck said, his face hardening. "Maybe it won't happen again — not to any of the women."

Bessie laughed. "You're funning yourself, mister! Them two don't know no other way to treat a woman. Beating just comes natural to them . . . And you telling me they're letting Jenny go still don't sound right. I'm betting they stop her."

"And I'll lay odds that they don't even try," Shawn said, smiling, but there was a firmness in his tone that belied any humor.

Bessie studied him briefly, then rose. Going to the kitchen, she obtained a small pot of coffee. Returning it to the table, she again sat down.

"Well, I'll be hoping for the best," she said, refilling his cup. "But dealing with them two's like playing patty-cake with a couple of rattlesnakes. Just can't ever be sure of anything."

Starbuck took a sip of the hot coffee. "You known McGraw a long time?"

"Longer'n anybody around here, I suspect."

"Maybe you've got some idea then who it is that's coming to kill him."

"Sure — ten, maybe twenty different men. Could be even more, considering all the places he's been and the enemies he's made."

"Not much help there. Way it is, I don't know who to watch for."

"And you probably won't until it's too late."

"Something I'd like to avoid. Got him and Fisher to agree to make every man check his gun when he comes into the Palace. Ought to help some."

"Ain't you never heard of sleeve guns and belly guns, Marshal? Be a plenty of them walking around armed just the same as if they was packing a pistol in a holster."

"I realize that, and it's the big reason why I need some kind of an idea who the killer might be."

Bessie stared out through the window. The man who had ridden in earlier was coming out of the stable, bending his steps

148

toward the restaurant.

"I'd like to help, Marshal, but I sure don't have no ideas. Like I said, Amos's made a passel of enemies — and that's a God's fact. The Palace ain't the first big, fancy house he's put up and run. Been three, maybe four just like it in other towns — and a man can't spit and tromp on folks like he's done all his life and get away with it forever."

"You with him in the other places?"

The woman nodded, her gaze now reaching out across the prairie. "Yeh, I was," she said in a faraway voice. "There was a time when I was like Jenny, all the other girls . . . Young and pretty — just as pretty as that one he brung in from Dodge —"

"Expect you were."

Bessie turned to him at once and gave him a wide smile. "I'm obliged to you for saying that — even if maybe you are just being polite . . . You must've had a fine up-bringing."

Shawn sloshed the coffee in his cup about absently. "They were fine people. I owe them a lot."

"They gone now?"

"Yes, only my brother and me are left — and I'm not sure about him. Sometimes I think he's dead, too."

"But being the kind you are, you just go right on hunting him," the woman said, a note of admiration in her voice. She twisted about and looked up at the rider entering the doorway. "Have yourself a seat, mister, I'll be right with you."

The man, dusty from what had evidently been a long ride, pulled off his hat. "No hurry, ma'm," he said as Bessie pulled herself upright. He shifted his attention to Starbuck. "Marshal?"

Shawn bobbed his head. "Something I can do for you?"

"Nope, it's something I can maybe do for you — if you're the one looking for a brother."

Starbuck came to quick alert. "That's me. What about my brother?"

"Well, was this a-way. I bumped into a fellow heading south last night, a piece east of here. About twenty mile or so. He asked me was I coming by here. I said yes, I sure was. He said I could do him and you a mighty big favor."

Starbuck nodded, waited impatiently for the rider to get to the point.

"He said when I got here to look you up first thing, tell you that this brother of your'n — Ben, I recollect he called him — was with a trail drive about ten mile north of where we was."

"Trail drive — this time of year?"

The rider grinned. "Same thing hit me, and I said so. Fellow went on to say it weren't no drive to Dodge or nothing like that. Was some rancher moving his herd . . . anyway, that's what I was to tell you, and I've done it."

Starbuck got to his feet, pulse quickening with each passing second . . . At last a direct lead on Ben — and a seemingly definite one at that. He extended his hand to the rider.

"Obliged to you, friend. I'll head out right now — about twenty miles east and ten north. I sure do appreciate your taking the trouble."

"Glad to help, Marshal," the man replied, and moved on to a table.

Shawn wheeled to Bessie. "When Red shows up, tell him what happened and say I'd like for him to sort of look after things for me until I get back. It ought to be around noon."

The woman smiled, her eyes bright with the same excitement that was rushing through him. "Sure thing — and good luck!"

17

All the long days and nights, all the lonely trails, the endless miles, the countless times he'd asked his question — perhaps such was coming to an end. The search could be over.

Shawn dared permit that thought to lodge firmly in his mind as he mounted the sorrel and rode from Babylon. Never before, after that first time when he had felt so certain he knew where Ben was and met disappointment instead, had he allowed himself the luxury of believing he had come to the end of the chase.

This time it was different. Word had been brought to him, and his brother had been called by name — not Damon Friend or some other alias, but Ben. That alone seemed proof enough.

He guessed the inquiries he had made at every opportunity had paid off after all. Time and again, when he had asked of Ben and received only empty stares and negative responses, he had felt he had simply wasted breath. But somewhere along the line someone had listened and remembered, and now he was on his way to meet the man he had sought for so long.

Starbuck took a deep breath and looked out over the vast Kansas prairie undulating gracefully as it stretched off to the horizon. The sun was up and warming the land from a clean, blue sky; larks wheeled and dipped above the bronzed grass, and the freshness of the day was as a tonic to him.

Forgotten were all the problems in Babylon: Jenny, Bart Fisher, Amos McGraw, and the killer he would one day have to face in the man's behalf. Ben and the need to see him again, renew their acquaintance and persuade him to his way of thinking — that was the matter to be considered. Babylon and all its troubles would still be there waiting when he returned.

Evidently Ben was working for some rancher. He likely would be surprised when he learned of their father's death and that he had been the object of a long search. Too, Ben must be made to realize the importance of returning to Muskingum with him and settling the estate. Ben would agree. His quarrel had been with old Hiram, and he should bear no ill feeling toward anyone else . . . Besides, if he was doing ordinary cowhand work, he would welcome his share of the estate.

It could be, if they hit it off well, and there was no reason they shouldn't as they had always gotten along, they might pool the cash they would be receiving — somewhat over thirty thousand dollars — and go into the cattle-raising business as partners.

He knew of several fine spreads that could be bought at a reasonable price, or if they so decided, they could start from scratch and build their ranch from the ground up. Riding across country as he had been doing for so long, he had seen a lot of places, well watered and deep in rich grass, that would offer fine possibilities.

Together they — Shawn grinned self-consciously as some of Hiram Starbuck's hard-surfaced practicability reclaimed him, forced him to put such thoughts from his mind. What the hell — Ben could be one with not the slightest desire to become a rancher. He could prefer to take his share of the money and just drift about, seeing all the country he had missed, visiting towns he had never gone to, and living a life of ease.

He himself had had enough wandering.

He was ready to settle down on a place of his own and think about a wife and a family and the warm comforts and complete satisfaction of a home of his own. Too many times he had pulled up on the crest of a hill, with the quiet, dark night all around him, and looked down at the lighted windows of some man's personal castle and felt the sharp stab of loneliness and the feeling of being cut off, of being apart — the only man in a vast, silent world. He had had his fill of that; once he received his share of the estate, that way of life was over.

He was obligated to return to Babylon, and he reckoned the thing to do was set up plans for a meeting there with Ben. He would return then to the Palace, fulfill his promise to Jenny, and advise McGraw and Fisher that he was pulling out, that they should find themselves a new lawman.

It was only right that he stay on the job until they located a replacement, however, but he guessed Ben would not object to hanging around a place like the Palace for a few days . . . Hell — there was the answer as to how he could get Jenny to Dodge City! Instead of asking Red, he would get Ben to make the trip.

Starbuck pulled up short. On a distant

slope he caught sight of a broad, dark mass gliding slowly along under the bright sun. A lump crowded into his throat. He swallowed hard. There was the herd . . . and Ben. . . .

Roweling the sorrel, he broke the big gelding into a fast lope, angling toward the riders he could see near the front of the cattle. One of them would be the owner or the trail boss; time would be saved by going first to him, asking where Ben could be found.

The men halted, wheeled to face him as he pounded across the last draw and raced toward them. One, an elderly individual with a handlebar mustache, considered him with puzzled blue eyes as he drew up.

"Name's Starbuck," Shawn said, nodding. "Looking for my brother."

The older man bobbed his head. "And mine's Wilson, and I sure don't know nobody named Starbuck."

The two punchers siding him laughed. Wilson favored them with a slow glance, then said, "Better keep after them cows, boys . . . I'll be along." He came back then to Shawn. "What makes you think this brother of your'n's around here?"

A tightness filled Starbuck as the edge of anticipation dulled. "I was told he was.

Name's Ben — Ben Starbuck. Or he could be calling himself Damon Friend."

The rancher gave the names deep thought. Finally, he shook his head. "Somebody must've been funning you. Ain't nobody by them handles working for me."

The stiffness in Shawn's throat made his words sound harsh. "I was sure he'd be here —"

"Well, he ain't."

"Yours the only herd moving across here?"

"Only one," Wilson said. "Marketing's all done with. This is some stock I bought from a fellow down in New Mexico. Got 'em cheap or I sure wouldn't be making no drive this time of year. Too dang dry . . . Who was it said you'd find your brother with my outfit?"

Starbuck shifted wearily on his saddle. He had acted like a kid. He had jumped and run without asking any questions of the man who had brought him the message.

"I never got his name. Just told me a fellow had stopped him on the trail, asked him to carry word to me. I'm the marshal in Babylon."

Wilson grinned. "I know the place. Been there once, and I sure ain't ever going back. Cost me nigh upwards of a thousand dollars to find out I couldn't beat that chuck-a-luck game . . . Sure a passel of mighty pretty females hanging around there, howsomever."

Shawn was barely listening. As the first surge of bitter disappointment, tempered fortunately by many previous and similar experiences, began to dwindle and cold reason take over, the wonder of why he had been sent on a long, useless ride crowded into his mind. Who had gone to such pains — and for what reason? Was it only that someone was playing a joke on him?

Perhaps, but he doubted it. Those who knew of his intense search for Ben would realize he would not take kindly to such a hoax and forego the idea . . . Of course there were those like Tom Gannon who might like to get back at him, but Starbuck's thoughts came to a standstill. Could it have been a plan to get him out of Babylon? Could that be the purpose underlying his fruitless ride? If so, who was responsible for it?

The answer to that came quickly: Amos McGraw's killer.

18

Starbuck brought his attention back to the rancher. "I think I know what this is all about," he said. "It was just a trick."

Wilson leaned forward on his saddle, resting his muscles. "Well, one thing I sure know. I ain't never had nobody with them names riding for me. What's this here brother of your'n look like?"

"Probably some like me. He could be shorter, maybe heavier."

"Don't help none, either. Was I to run into a fellow like that, what'll I tell him?"

"That I'm looking for him," Shawn answered; then he paused, giving the matter thought. After a moment he continued. "I doubt if I'll be around Babylon much longer. You do come across Ben, say I'll be in Santa Fe, to look me up there."

"Sure will," the rancher said. "Luck."

Shawn nodded and swung around, the belief that he had been purposely drawn away from the settlement now a conviction with him. It was the only logical explanation for what had happened. Digging spurs into the gelding, he pointed the big horse west. He could only hope that his return would not be too late.

He rode into Babylon around midday, the sorrel breathing hard and showing sweat from the fast ride. A dozen or so men were gathered on the gallery of the Palace, and as he swept up to the rack, all wheeled to meet him.

"Been a killing, Marshal!" a man in the front shouted as he swung from the saddle.

"McGraw?"

The rider's face showed surprise. He bobbed his head. "How'd you know?"

Starbuck swore quietly. He had been right. It had been a plan to get him out of the way; by his leaving he had left Amos McGraw at the mercy of the killer . . . He had failed the man — regardless of what he thought of him, he had failed him, had fallen down on his job.

"Guessed," he replied in a wooden voice, and hurried up onto the gallery.

"That ain't all," another voice called after him. "Fisher's bad shot up, too. Doc says he ain't going to make it." Fisher . . . He hadn't been one marked for death. Evidently he had gotten in the way. "Anybody know who did it?"

The man who had spoken first said, "It was that redheaded friend of yours — we think," he replied, and then, eyes narrowing thoughtfully, fell silent.

Red — McGraw's killer!

Shawn felt the impact of that information as forcibly as if he had been struck across the face. He shook his head. *We think,* the rider had said. They weren't sure.

He turned again to the crowd intending to ask another question, but hesitated as he read the suspicion on their faces. They were wondering if he and the redhead had arranged the matter, if he had conveniently absented himself from Babylon in order for Red to have a clear opportunity.

"You can forget what you've got in your minds," he snapped. "I had no part in it. Where's Red now?"

"He got away, riding south. Think maybe he's got lead in him. The bartender — Pete Dison — got off a shot when he run for it."

"Anybody go after him?"

"Nope. Weren't nobody that anxious to get hisself shot. Besides, we was all waiting for you — you being the marshal."

Shawn moved on into the strangely dark and silent Palace. He crossed the deserted floor, heels echoing hollowly on the boards, and made his way to the office in the rear where he could see several men and women gathered. At his approach they all pulled back, allowed him to enter. Pete greeted him with a solemn nod.

"Glad you're back. Reckon you've heard what happened?"

"I was told. How's Fisher?"

"Dying slow. Ain't got a chance . . . You find your brother? Bessie told us where you'd gone."

"It was only a trick to get me out of town. McGraw do any talking before he died?"

"Wasn't in no shape to. Three slugs — killed him right off."

Shawn glanced about at the sullen, accusing faces turned to him. McGraw was not liked, was even hated by most, but he was dead, and they blamed him. And in the eyes of some he saw also the same suspicion he had recognized outside on the Palace's porch. Shrugging, he pushed that disturbing realization to the back of his mind and wheeled to Dison.

"They told me it was Red who did it — or that you think it was."

"Pretty sure, Marshal," the barman replied. "Didn't get no good look at him. Reckon nobody did. I was the only one that seen the killer riding off down the alley. Grabbed up McGraw's pistol, got me off a shot. Either hit him or his horse."

"Then you're not sure . . . Know what happened?"

"Can't say much about it. Was just after we closed down this morning. I expect you'd just rode off, judging from what Bessie said. I was behind the bar doing some fixing and heard somebody start shooting back upstairs in McGraw's room.

"I run up there in a hurry. About halfways up the stairs I heard a couple of more shots. I sort of hung back then a bit, not knowing what I was getting into. Some of the girls was yelling, too, and a bunch of the customers was coming in from the street.

"I went on then, and the first thing I seen when I got up on the balcony was Bart laying there at Amos's door. Seems he heard the shooting, too, went to see what was going on, and got himself plugged."

"Red — or whoever it was doing the shooting — was he still in McGraw's room?"

"No, he'd jumped out the window and

dropped to the ground. He had his horse waiting right below, I guess. I seen Amos was dead so I grabbed up his iron and run to the window. Fellow was legging it out fast. I shot at him, but like I said, I ain't for sure I hit him."

"And you couldn't tell for certain that it was Red?"

"No, I can't swear it, but I think so."

"Anybody looked around town to see if he's still here?"

The bartender shook his head. "Ain't nobody seen him . . . And they say his horse is gone."

Starbuck looked down. There could be an explanation for the redhead's absence, of course; he could have ridden out early on some errand, or possibly he had simply decided to move on, but Shawn found such reasoning thin and hard to accept. Everything pointed to the redhead, and if true, then he had been in Babylon all the time, had just waited until McGraw, feeling safe again, had returned . . . And Red, feeling the ties of friendship and not wanting to involve him in a shoot-out, had arranged for the message that had taken him out of town and away from trouble.

"You're going after him, ain't you, Marshal?" one of the dealers asked. "It was

164

murder, no matter how you look at it — and you're the law."

"I'll go after whoever did it," Starbuck replied. "I first got to know who the man was. I'd like to talk to Fisher if —"

Gilman came into the room, his features stern. "Bart Fisher's dead," he announced in a businesslike tone, facing Starbuck. "Regained consciousness near the end. He said to tell you the killer was Red — your friend."

Shawn drew up slowly. It was true then. There could be no doubt since Fisher barely knew the redhead and would have no reason to lie.

"Something else he told me, said to pass on," the physician continued, transferring his attention to the others. "It wasn't known, but Bessie is Amos McGraw's lawful wife. He hasn't had anything to do with her for years, but he let her hang around so's she wouldn't starve — as long as she never told anybody about the connection . . . She's owner of Babylon now, and you're all working for her."

Starbuck heard the murmur that ran through the crowd, felt a start of surprise as he turned away. He understood Bessie now — her harsh words and defiant attitude. But the thought was fleeting. Foremost now in his mind was Red and the obligation he had to go after the man who was his friend and bring him to justice.

"You want some help, Marshal?" Dison asked as he walked off. "I can get up a posse real quick."

"No, best I do it alone."

There was a long breath of silence, and then a voice in the crowd said, "You sure you aim to bring him back?"

Shawn halted, came around slowly. His features were set, grim.

"I'm sure," he said quietly, and moved on.

19

The sorrel had been tired from the morning's trip, and Starbuck fearing the possibility of a hard chase, took time to draw a fresh horse from the stable. Mounting he rode from Babylon, pointing south, the direction that all agreed Red had taken.

He was finding it hard to accept the facts — that the redhead was the killer, that he had been duped by him. But there was no avoiding it; Pete Dison had been fairly sure, and Fisher's dying statement had made it positive.

When he really thought about it, he guessed he had no valid reason to question it. He scarcely knew Red, had met him more or less by accident in the Palace that evening when he had been braced by Hake Dallman and his crowd. After that they had spoken together, had a few meals in Bessie's café — and that was it.

He could see now that Red had intentionally held their friendship to a minimum, knowing that he would kill Amos McGraw at the first good opportunity; aware that Shawn was paid to prevent the very act he planned to commit, he made certain their acquaintanceship did not grow into one of proportions.

Starbuck appreciated that, but it could make no difference in what he must do. The badge he wore was real, one recognized by the county and by the state of Kansas as well. With it came the duty all lawmen accepted: An outlaw must be brought to justice regardless of identity or circumstances. If an exception was to be made, the law would make it. Such was not up to the discretion of the man wearing the star.

Perhaps Red had good reason to kill. Fisher's, of course, was unplanned and came about when the gambler sought to interfere. McGraw had died for something out of the past, and his death had certainly been carefully plotted.

The reason, whatever its nature, might have a bearing on a judge's final decision, once Red stood trial. It could be that he was justified in killing Amos McGraw, and possibly Bart Fisher, also — both of whom undoubtedly had done much in their lifetimes to deserve such fate . . . But Red's reason would need to be a good one — and again, it was the law that would make that determination.

Shawn's thoughts were dark as he rode steadily south on the tough little buckskin he had chosen. The prints of Red's horse had not been hard to pick up. He had spotted the marks — a deep-set trail made by a fast-running mount — coming out of the alley and leading south almost at once.

A mile or so below the settlement, Red had veered onto the main road, apparently realizing that his horse could travel faster on its firm, well-beaten soil than on the less solid footing of open country.

If the redhead's mount had been shot, it showed little evidence of it so far, Starbuck decided, and reckoned it had been the man himself who had been wounded if Pete's aim had been good.

But a time later it became obvious that the animal had gone lame and was slowing its pace. Shawn roweled the buckskin to a faster lope, and shortly, with the sun beginning to drop low in the west, he crested a rise and drew to a quick halt.

Before him on the powdery earth were the hard-set prints of a man's boots along with the tracks of a horse. Close by were several dark splotches in the loose soil . . . Red's mount had been hit. He had stood up under the wound until he had labored to the top of the hill. There he had been forced to stop.

The redhead had dismounted, done what he could for the suffering animal, and finally ridden on — still miles from Brewer's Flat, if that was his destination.

Shawn, his reading of the signs finished, shaded his eyes against the slanting rays of the sun and swept the distance with a probing gaze. Far ahead a dark mass laid a small scar on the gray-green flank of another rise . . . It could be a patch of brush different in color from anything nearby, or it could be the redhead's horse, finally dead.

Going quickly to the saddle, Starbuck again searched the country with squinted eyes, hoping to get from that somewhat higher elevation a better view and possibly catch sight of a lone figure cutting across the low hills.

But the land, except for the dark mass, was deserted, and spurring the buckskin, he rode on, hopeful now of sighting his objective in the empty sameness before darkness fell and brought an additional problem. If such did occur, he decided, he would have no recourse other than to hurry on to Brewer's Flat and station himself between it and the direction from which Red would come.

Reaching that point too late to make an interception would give rise to even larger problems — ones that would be difficult to solve . . . But he would face them if and when the time came. He would concentrate now on overtaking his man before such could happen.

It was Red's horse.

The bay had been shot in the hip. The wound had been only ordinary, and likely the animal could have recovered if he had not been compelled to continue, had instead been given some attention. But Red had no choice; he had ridden the bay as far as he could go, and when the animal had finally dropped, he had continued on foot.

How long ago? Shawn dropped to the ground beside the horse. Kneeling, he placed a hand on its neck. Faintly warm . . . Red, walking in boots meant only for riding, could not be far. That he had moved on hurriedly was indicated by the fact that he had not paused to remove his gear and take it with him . . . It meant also that he was aware of the rider on his trail.

Leading the buckskin, Shawn crossed to the edge of the small plateau and carefully went over the ground until he located a heel mark of Red's boots. The earth there was hard and gravelly where the winds and rains had long since swept away the topsoil, but by patient persistence he found enough of the arched imprints to tell him that the husky redhead had struck out on a direct southeast line across the prairie.

Starbuck climbed back onto the buckskin, threw a side glance to the west. An hour or so of daylight remained. He must act quickly or the advantage would swing to Red. He shifted his eyes then to the gear on the dead horse. The boot was empty. The man would be armed with both rifle and six gun. He had taken his canteen, also, and was prepared to make a stand if need be.

Again Shawn swept the country before him. He had reached the area of heavy-browed buttes that lay this side of Brewer's Flat, and spotting Red would now be a difficult task — even if daylight prevailed. It would be wiser to abandon pursuit, as such, follow the alternate plan he had of placing himself between his man and the outlaw settlement, position himself in the advantageous spot, and let Red come to him.

The decision made, Starbuck cut away from the little plateau, swinging west to get the hill behind him, and began a fast circling to the south. He angled wide of the first line of buttes, doubling back finally when he judged he had put a good five miles between himself and the area where Red most likely would be.

He rode more cautiously from there, holding the buckskin to a brisk walk, choosing the swales and washes that kept him below the horizon and the horse in the loose sand where hoof beats would be muffled.

The prospect of coming face to face with Red, of likely having to shoot it out with him became more disturbing as he closed in to set up his ambush. He had liked the redhead even though he had known him but a short period. In that brief time, however, Red had become as near a close friend as he had ever had, and the probability of being forced to kill the man, even in the line of duty, was weighing heavily on Shawn's mind.

It had to be done — either capture or kill, his own feelings notwithstanding. He could only hope that Red would not put up a fight, would surrender himself and return willingly. It was a faint hope, Shawn knew; Red was a desperate man, likely would never throw down his weapons.

Starbuck halted the buckskin. A broad, sandy arroyo well studded with brush clumps lay before him, one that curved down from the higher hills and buttes to the west. Red would be following the wash; it would afford the easiest and most direct route, from the point where his horse had gone, down to Brewer's Flat.

He glanced around. Shadows were lengthening. Darkness was not far off. He could set up his watch here, be well hidden by the brush while still having a good view of the arroyo. A man coming down it would be quickly visible even in the half-light of the stars.

Swinging from the saddle, Shawn tethered the buckskin a safe distance back from the edge of the wash and, returning to the low bank, set to arranging a spot for himself in the brushy fringe. Grasping the stalk of a fairly large clump, he wrenched it free of its mooring and moved to place it in a barren gap that required covering.

The dry scrape of a branch against cloth brought him around. His hand swept down for the gun on his hip, came up fast.

Red, rifle leveled, stood before him. Evidently he had just passed that point chosen by Starbuck for ambush, had heard a rider come in, and had cut back, probably with the idea in mind of getting a much-needed horse for himself.

A long sigh slipped from the redhead's lips as he shook his head. "I was hoping it wouldn't be you," he said heavily.

20

Etched against the pale light of dusk, Starbuck held himself motionless. Red, now utterly silent, remained equally unmoving. For a long, breathless half-minute the two figures, poised like tempered steel springs needing only a touch to uncoil and lash out, hung there in the fading day, eyes locked, guns leveled in a deadly standoff.

And then abruptly the weapon in the husky redhead's hands wavered. "The hell with it," he murmured in a worn, frustrated voice, and tossed the rifle to the ground at Starbuck's feet.

Shawn's tense body eased. Stepping down into the arroyo, he reached out, took Red's pistol from its holster, and thrust it under the waistband of his pants. Putting away his own weapon, he faced the man. There was relief in his eyes, a thankfulness in his heart that the redhead had chosen not to resist.

"I hate this," he said. "I wish, too, that it could have been somebody else."

Red nodded woodenly.

"Is what they say true — that you killed McGraw and Fisher?"

Again the husky rider moved his head up and down. "Bart got in the way. I wasn't gunning for him — only McGraw. They both dead?"

"Both of them. Means a murder charge."

"What I expected — but I sure as hell ain't sorry, not for cutting down McGraw, anyway."

Shawn studied the man thoughtfully. "Who hired you to kill him?"

"Nobody — was a personal matter." Red turned away, then moved to the edge of the arroyo and sat down on the grassy, littered bank. "Fact is, McGraw didn't even know me."

Starbuck, arms folded across his chest, continued to study the redhead. His face sagged with weariness, and the film of dust lying upon it turned him gray and old looking.

"Expect you could use some grub."

Red looked up, hopefully. "Drink of whiskey'd do more of a job."

Shawn grinned. "Can't help you there. How about coffee?"

"I'll settle for that — and don't bother about grub. Not hungry."

Starbuck crossed to where he had picketed the buckskin. Unfastening the left pocket of his saddlebags, he obtained his sack of coffee and the lard tin and cup he regularly packed. Adding his canteen of water, he returned to the wash.

Red had not stirred, simply remained stonily motionless on the bank of the arroyo. His eyes followed Shawn as he gathered a pile of dry branches and leaves, built a fire, and set the tin filled with water over the flames.

"Reckon you're wondering what it's all about," he said then.

Starbuck did not raise his glance. "I know all I need to — that you were the one who killed McGraw and Fisher. The reason why is something for a judge to hear."

"I'd like for you to know the whole thing, too. I figure you for a friend of mine and entitled to it."

Shawn added another handful of wood to the fire. The darting tongues leaped higher around the lard tin, setting the water to simmering and spiraling a column of smoke up into the dwindling light in the sky.

"Up to you," he said.

"Name's Quist — Dan Quist," Red said. "It ain't often I'm called by it, but that's what it is. Home's in Arkansas, little place close to the Louisiana line. Folks had a farm there. There wasn't much left to it after the war, but my brother and me — he was a bit younger — we'd just about got it back in shape when the trouble started."

Quist leaned forward, rested himself, elbows on knees. Starbuck waited, continued to work with the fire.

"Began when Billy — my brother — married a girl we'd sort of grown up with. Name was Ellie — for Ellen, I think. Her people had a place north of us . . . She was the prettiest little thing I've ever seen — all bright eyed and rosy cheeked and put together the way that makes a man stop and turn around for a second look when she passed by.

"Well, they took themselves a honeymoon. Went to New Orleans right soon after they was married, and it was while they was there that McGraw seen her. He had himself a place outside of town — one like the Babylon Palace, big and fancy and with a stable of pretty women on hand to keep the customers coming."

"Sounds like the same kind of a deal,"

Starbuck observed, reaching for his neck-erchief.

Making a pad of the folded cloth, he lifted the tin of boiling water off the flames and set it aside. Taking up the sack of crushed coffee beans, he poured a generous handful into the container, returned it to the fire, placing it slightly to one side so that it could simmer without boiling over.

"It was," Red continued. "The second day Billy and his wife were in New Orleans, she disappeared. Just plain dropped out of sight. He hunted everywhere, even went to the police, but they couldn't find her, either. Was like she'd stepped into a deep hole."

The coffee surged up. Shawn removed it again; taking up a twig, he stirred down the froth and sat back to let it cool.

"Billy wrote me about it finally. I packed up and went there fast as I could, then the two of us started hunting Ellie, one going one direction, the other taking another. Was about a month later I just happened to go into McGraw's place — after a drink. I was standing at the bar and I looked around and there Ellie was. She was coming across the floor, all painted up and dressed in mostly nothing, with some

180

jasper hanging onto her arm. She seen me, too. Her eyes turned big, and a funny kind of look — pure shame — come over her. She turned and run up the stairs to where the women had their rooms."

Shawn took up the cooled tin, poured the cup full of the strong liquid, and handed it to Red. Cradling the container in his palms, he stared into it.

"It wasn't hard to figure what had happened. McGraw had grabbed her — kidnapped her, actually — and forced her to become one of his brothel women, same way as he kept the Babylon Palace stocked. After a few days I reckon she was too ashamed to leave the place and go back to Billy."

Quist took a long drink from his cup. Starbuck, compelled to use the lard tin, sampled the dark brew thoughtfully.

"Is that why you came after McGraw?"

"Only the start of it. I — I made a mistake. I shouldn't have told Billy I'd found her. I know now it would've been better to just let it pass — but I did tell him, and he went there to get her. Ellie seen him coming and shot herself.

"Billy went plumb crazy then. He got himself a gun and started after McGraw, but somebody warned McGraw. When my

181

brother walked into the saloon, McGraw stepped up behind him and put a bullet in his back — killed him."

"Murder," Starbuck murmured. "Police sure should've taken a hand then."

"Hell, the police always moves too slow. By the time they got on it McGraw had pulled out. He'd sold his half interest in the place to his partner and run for it. Just disappeared."

"And that's when you started out to track him down —"

Quist nodded and finished off the last of his coffee. "First I took Billy and Ellie back to the farm and buried them in the family graveyard where we'd put my folks. Then I took off. All I wanted was to find Amos McGraw and kill him. At first it was because of what he'd done to Ellie and my brother, and then it got to be a sort of — of —"

"Crusade?"

"Yeh, that's it. McGraw made it a business of putting young girls to work for him. If he couldn't talk them into it, he'd just grab them, make them do it anyway, and pretty soon my need to square things for Billy and Ellie got all mixed up with an idea that I had to kill McGraw and keep him from ruining the lives of any more girls."

"How long ago did this begin?"

"Going on five years now. He was hard to run down, had a couple of other places in the time between New Orleans and Babylon. I almost got him at one —"

Shawn frowned, stared into the fire. "If he saw you then, why didn't he recognize you in Babylon?"

"Never seen my face. I was wearing a flour sack with holes cut in it for eyes. I told him then I'd been hunting him and that I'd made up my mind to kill him if it took the rest of my life. Was right about there that a couple of his hunkies jumped me from behind. He ducked out, scared, leaving it for them to finish me off. I got away from them before they could find out who I was. When McGraw learned that, he moved on again.

"It was quite a while later when I heard about the Palace. Rode there in a hurry, but again he'd got wind of me coming and had pulled out, but he decided to only hole up and hire a fast gun — you — to take care of me, this time instead of running. Didn't work for him. I got to him anyway."

Dan Quist fell silent, his gaze lost in the darkness beyond the flare of the dwindling fire. Finally, "Not sorry for one minute that I killed him, Shawn — only sorry that

I had to play a mean trick on you to do it. Feel I had plenty of reasons to put a bullet in him. Man like McGraw ain't entitled to live on this earth with decent folks . . . You agree with that?"

Starbuck nodded slowly.

"Then, the way it looks to me, I've done the country a big favor, and there ain't no reason why I should have to go to jail and stand trial for something that wasn't no crime . . . You agree with me there, too?"

21

Shawn mulled the words of Dan Quist about in his mind. There was truth in them — he could not deny that. The world was a better place without men like Amos McGraw. They were a blight, a curse that mankind should not be compelled to bear — but to judge another human being, regardless of what he had done, was wrong; such had been drilled into him time and again by his mother as well as by flint-edged old Hiram.

"It's not how I feel about it that counts," he said slowly. "It's what the law says —"

"The law!" Red broke in impatiently. "Where was the law when Billy was murdered? Took their goddam time getting on the matter — time that let McGraw run — go free!"

"Can't blame the law for that. It was the man or men in charge of it that failed."

"They were friends of his, all of them. They'd been bought off."

"Which only proves what I said. It wasn't the law at fault but the kind of men representing it . . . And they'd be the exception. Most lawmen are honest and try to do their job."

Quist's pale eyes locked in on Starbuck. "Like you?"

Shawn nodded. "Like me."

"But you ain't even a real lawman!"

"Afraid you're wrong. McGraw and Fisher had the authority to hire a marshal — even hold court."

"You forget I was there when you took the job? Hell, you wasn't even sworn in — no oath or anything."

"It works out the same. I accepted the oath and all it meant whether I spoke it or not. Far as I'm concerned there's no difference."

Dan Quist shrugged. "I always heard you couldn't cheat an honest man. Reckon there's no talking one out of his principles, either . . . There any of that coffee left?"

Starbuck picked up his canteen, poured a small amount of water into the lard tin, and set it back over the fire. The flames had dwindled to a scatter of small tongues. He tossed another handful of sticks into the graying embers and fanned them with his hat.

"Be a couple of minutes."

"No hurry," Red replied. "I got plenty of time, all the rest of my life, I guess. Where'll you be taking me? No sense going back to Babylon."

"Dodge City. The marshal there's my friend. His name's Earp. Sort of owes me a favor. He'll see that you get a fair shake."

Red wagged his head. "Ain't much for hoping."

"I figure a judge will listen to you — and he'll know all about McGraw and Fisher. It was in Dodge that I heard about Babylon and the kind of place it was, so you won't need to convince him of what McGraw really was."

"You going to take a hand in it — as a witness, maybe?"

"I aim to tell what I think — that you're my friend and you figured you had a right and a reason to do what you did."

Quist rubbed at his jaw. "I'll appreciate that. Expect it'll count for plenty."

"I figure to tell the judge how you sided me in getting back the money that Dallman and his bunch stole, too. It should prove to him that you're no outlaw."

Red nodded. "Anything you say in my favor will be good — and I'll be beholden to you for it . . . That coffee ought to be done by now," he added, holding out his cup.

Shawn emptied the lard tin into the container, blocking the coarse grounds with a bit of wood placed along the tin's rim.

"Anyway, however it comes out," Quist said, easing back, "I reckon it won't matter too much. I rode a few thousand miles to do what I had to, and now it's all over. Long ago I learned to take what comes, just live one day at a time — same as you're doing, hunting for your brother. You take it a day at a time."

"No point looking ahead until I do catch up with him . . . I thought I'd come to the end of that when I got the word you'd sent me by that drifter."

"I hated to fool you, but it was the only way I could see to get you out of town. I'm telling you again I'm sorry I fired you all up and let you get hurt."

"I'm used to it," Shawn said, rising and staring out over the moonlight flooded prairie. "If I'd taken time to think it over when I got the message, I'd figured there was nothing to it."

"Probably, but you'd have gone just the same — just on the maybe there was some truth to it. That's the way a man's head works. Guess there's some kind of hope in him that keeps pushing him along no matter what . . . You had any leads at all on your brother since you came to Babylon?"

Starbuck shook his head. "None. I spread the word around, and about everybody's trying to remember if he might've dropped by."

"Seems he would, was he in this part of the country. Expect I've finished things there for you now. Place'll probably shut down."

"I doubt it. Turns out that Bessie was McGraw's wife. Fisher told that to Doc Gilman before he died. She'll likely take over and keep it running."

Red's face was blank with astonishment. "Old Bessie was McGraw's real wife?"

"So Fisher said. Always sort of wondered about her. Once told me she'd known McGraw longer than anybody else around — and she sure never minded saying what she thought of him."

"Funny she never told nobody about it."

"Afraid of him for one thing — and it was plain she hated him. Could be she was hanging on, waiting for the day when she could get back at him."

"Well, I beat her to that," Quist said with a short laugh. "We staying here till morning?"

"No, best we head back pretty soon. We're going to have to ride double, and it'll be easier on the horse traveling while it's cool."

"How about Babylon — we swinging by there?"

"Got to. You need a horse. It's only place we can get one."

Quist wagged his head. "I doubt if I'm going to be very popular around there."

"Nobody'll bother us, not when I tell them I'm taking you to Dodge. No reason for locking you up in Babylon. McGraw was the judge, and he's dead."

"Whatever you say. Be obliged to you, however, if you'll keep your iron handy — just in case some of that bunch around the Palace gets lynching ideas."

"I'll watch sharp —"

"You ain't about to do nothing," Hake Dallman drawled from the shadows, " 'cept raise your hands, real careful like . . . Me and the boys was headed for Babylon to pay you a little visit. Spotting your fire's saved us a long ride."

22

Rigid in the quick, hushed tension, mentally cursing himself for his carelessness, Starbuck raised his arms. Quist, remaining seated on the bank of the arroyo, followed suit.

Shawn didn't know if the redhead realized it or not, but an avenue of escape had opened for him. When the outlaws discovered he was a prisoner en route to a cell, the chances were good they would welcome him into the fold, the incident at Brewer's Flat notwithstanding. Now being on the opposite side of the law would make a vast difference.

Dallman emerged from the dense brush to the left and sauntered in close to the fire. The others appeared. Weapons leveled, they fanned out to either side of him. Starbuck eyed them coldly . . . Al, three of the bunch who had been in on the robbery, and Gannon, the gunslinger he had so recently driven out of Babylon.

Smirking, Dallman hooked his thumbs in his belt, thrust his head forward. "Yes sir, sure makes it mighty nice, finding you birds here . . . Get their irons, Al."

The scarred man crossed to Red, then drew up in surprise. Frowning, he wheeled. Jerking Starbuck's pistol from its holster, he pointed to Red's weapon thrust under Shawn's waistband.

"Would you look here! I think the marshal's got hisself a prisoner."

Dallman stepped forward and claimed the redhead's gun. Holding it in front of Quist, he said, "This your'n?"

Red nodded.

"He trotting you back to the pokey?"

Again the husky rider moved his head.

"Figured you and him was pals . . . What for?"

"A killing," Red said, slowly lowering his hands.

Dallman's interest heightened. "That a fact? Who?"

"McGraw and Bart Fisher."

The outlaw's jaw sagged. "Well, what do you know! You sure picked yourself a couple of real humdingers. Why'd you do it?"

Quist had come to his feet. His shoulders twitched. "They was a couple of bastards that needed killing."

Hake Dallman glanced at the men ranged behind Starbuck. "Ain't saying they didn't, but that don't make me forget something — it was you that blasted the Kid."

"Couldn't help it," Red replied coolly. "It was him or me — and he was a damned fool to try for his gun."

The outlaw considered that briefly. "Yeh, reckon that's right. Kid wasn't long on sense, anyhow."

Starbuck, with Hake standing an arm's length in front of him, calculated the odds. It would be easy to grab the outlaw, pin his arms to his body, and whirl to one side. But the chances of his being able to do so fast enough before the others could act were small. Likely he would get a half a dozen bullets in his back before he could complete the move and snatch up a gun.

But he must come up with something. Dallman and his bunch intended to kill him where he stood, and with Dan Quist evidently going over, joining them, he would have to depend upon himself.

"I got to get myself a horse," he heard Red say. "Mine's laying back up the trail a piece, dead. One of you mind me riding double till we get to Brady's? I figure I can dicker him out of something."

"Reckon so but there ain't no use'n that," Dallman said. "The marshal won't be needing his no more. Whyn't you just help yourself to the one he's forking?"

Quist, grinning, shook his head. "I sure never thought of that," he said, and turned to look at the buckskin picketed back in the brush.

In that same instant he bent forward. Starbuck caught the faint glint of metal as he snatched up the rifle he had tossed there earlier, saw him spin fast. The weapon smashed the quiet of the night with its shocking report. Hake Dallman recoiled as the heavy bullet drove into him and knocked him to the ground.

Shawn lunged to one side as Red levered the rifle and threw himself full-length into the brush. The weapon spat again at the remaining outlaws scrambling for cover. A bullet whipped at him as Al triggered a shot. Starbuck, swearing at his own helplessness, glanced about for the pistol Dallman had been holding.

A dull shine in the sand drew his attention. It was Red's gun — the one he was looking for. Ducked low, he rushed from the protection of the stump behind which he had taken refuge, scooped up the weapon, and plunged on. A bullet whipped at his leg, another breathed hot against his cheek, others whirred close by.

He reached the bank of the arroyo, dived into the deep shadow of the brush lining it, and pulled himself around. In that same instant he saw the scar-faced Al dart into the open. He pressed off a quick shot and saw the outlaw stumble and fall.

The remaining members of the gang had pocketed themselves in a dense pool of blackness and undergrowth a short distance beyond. They were firing steadily, their guns marked by small flashes of orange each time discharged. The outlaws were taking similar advantage, were aiming their shots at the telltale flare of Quist's rifle and his six-gun.

"I'll circle around — come at them from the side," he called in a hoarse whisper to the redhead, a few strides below him. "They've got us spotted here . . . Hold your fire until I open up."

Red's answer was an unintelligible murmur. Starbuck, on hands and knees, worked back deeper into the brush until he was well away from the arroyo; then rising, he circled in toward the outlaws' left. They, too, had ceased their shooting, apparently now in doubt as to the location of their targets since they were drawing no answering shots.

Breathing hard, Shawn halted at the edge of a small clearing. The outlaws, he thought, were directly ahead in what looked to be a brush-filled hollow. He could not be sure, however, as their guns continued to remain silent. For a long minute he waited there, listening, hoping for a sound that would reveal the presence of the men. There was only the far-distant barking of a coyote.

Turned impatient, he moved through the dappling of moonlight filtering through the brush to a mound of roots and earth a stride or so above him. Crouching behind it, he held his pistol at arm's length to one side and squeezed off a shot into the hollow.

A splatter of answering bullets came immediately. Lead clipped through the brush surrounding him and thudded into the solid mass of soil and twisted roots. He rolled farther over, aimed again at the dark swale. The hammer of his weapon clicked on an empty cartridge.

Lying flat on his back, he emptied the spent casings from the weapon's cylinder and fed in a fresh supply. Snapping the loading gate shut, he rolled back into position and paused.

The quick tattoo of horses racing off into the night reached him. He remained motionless, listening, waiting until the sound had faded entirely, then slowly drew himself upright. The outlaws had pulled out. Even Gannon had turned tail and was running.

Shawn turned and headed back to where he had left Dan Quist. It came to him suddenly that the redhead had not opened up with his rifle as he had expected him to do. Ignoring the circuitous path he had followed to get at the outlaws' flank, Starbuck cut directly into the open, hurried by the lifeless figures of Al and Hake Dallman, and reached the brush where Quist had made his stand.

The redhead was sitting up, hunched forward, hands pressed to his middle. The rifle lay across his legs, and blood smeared its stock and metal action. Shawn knelt beside him.

"Bad?"

Quist looked up wearily. "Reckon so," he replied in a dragging voice. "We get them — all?"

"Dallman and Al. The others run for it."

"Best you — hightail it — out of — here . . . Could come back — trick you."

Quist began to sink. Starbuck slipped an

arm around his shoulders and laid him down gently.

"Red, there anything I can do — maybe take word —"

"No — ain't nobody — left . . . Better — this way . . . Less trouble — all around," the redhead murmured, and went limp.

Shawn studied the man's slack face for a long time. There was an ease to it now, almost a contentment as if he were pleased by the way it had all ended.

Slowly Starbuck pulled himself upright. He guessed it was better, if ever death is a better solution. Turning away, he moved off to retrieve the horses.

23

He loaded Quist's body on one of the two horses he found picketed back a distance from the arroyo and those of Hake Dallman and Al on the other. Then, astride his own buckskin, he pulled out of the broad wash and in the crisp, silvered night struck for Babylon.

They were not far from the settlement — less than half the distance separating the town from Buffalo Brady's outlaw sanctuary. Thus, he could expect to arrive sometime near first light.

That thought stirred little interest in Starbuck. Dan Quist's death had taken something out of him, and despite the fact the redhead was an admitted murderer, Shawn's feeling of friendship had diminished none. Red had done what, in his heart, he believed he must do; that in the doing he had flaunted the law was undeniable, but to him it was a justifiable action.

And who was to say he was not right? The system that threw a cloak of protection around criminals like Amos McGraw, that safeguarded them from earned retribution at the hands of one such as Dan Quist because it was the prerogative of that system to exact the ultimate punishment was not necessarily fair.

Vague technicalities, influence in high places, and the sheer power of money all too often stayed the mills of the gods and permitted the patently evil to flourish while the beset floundered helplessly, unable to find redress.

Quist had simply chosen not to be counted among those, Shawn realized, and while it went against everything he had been taught, and he could not condone the murders his redheaded friend had committed, he could understand his behavior.

But it was all water downstream now. Red would never stand before a judge and hear himself sentenced to death at the end of a hangman's rope or, at best, assigned to a cell within high prison walls for the remainder of his life. Amos McGraw and his lesser light, Bart Fisher, would not again set themselves up as kings in a regime of greed and lust, and the land was also freed of three, more conventional outlaws — the

Kid, Al, and Hake Dallman.

That much should be said for Dan Quist, regardless; in his vengeance-oriented search he had relieved the world of two stellar malefactors along with a trio of others that it could very well do without.

Starbuck drew to a halt on the brow of a hill, shrugged to dispel the heavy thoughts that filled his mind. Raising himself in his stirrups, he looked back over the land, stirring now with a night wind, that he had crossed — a remembrance of Red's last caution coming to him.

The prairie lay silent and deserted. There was no one on his trail. Hake Dallman's friends had evidently decided that their leader's quarrel was his own and that further prosecution of it was not their affair.

Sighing, he settled onto the leather, shifting his attention to the east. A pale flare of pearl was spreading across the dark arch of the sky. Dawn was not far off. He would be glad to see the sun again.

Touching the buckskin with his rowels, he moved on, riding before the breeze, idly listening now to the sounds and seeing the signs of life awakening to meet the new day . . . A rabbit poised in a sage clump, birds cheeping sleepily, an owl hooting his reluctance to yield the night.

Starbuck's head, slung forward at ease as he rocked to and fro in accord with the buckskin's rhythmic plodding, came up slowly. Miles ahead, slowly taking shape against the brightening sky, was a broad pall of smoke. He frowned. It was much too extensive a cloud for a range fire and he could recall no grove of trees in that area that would account for such a fire.

Babylon. . . .

The thought came to him in that next instant. The settlement was ablaze, was going or had already gone up in flames. There was no other explanation.

Spurring the buckskin to a lope and urging the two horses with their roped-down loads to keep pace, Starbuck dropped off the rise he had been following into a long swale and came finally to the road.

Swinging onto its firm surface, he maintained speed until he broke over the last hump and looked down onto the flat where the structures stood.

There was little of Babylon left. The fieldstone that had served as foundations for the buildings loomed starkly gray through the hovering layers of smoke and swirling ashes whipped about by the breeze. Here and there charred timbers silhouetted bleakly, marking a corner of the Palace, the entrance to the stable, the rear of the hotel . . . Even the Flophouse, quarters of the ill fortuned, was no more. The jail was a lonely cage.

Shocked, Starbuck turned his eyes to the clearing east of the smoking ruin. Two dozen or so persons, a number of horses, piles of belongings, and a wagon or two occupied it. Urging the buckskin on, he rode forward. As he approached, a few lifted stunned faces to him. Only Pete Dison, clothing scorched, brows and hair singed, stepped up to greet him.

Dropping from the saddle, Shawn glanced again at the smoldering skeleton. "How'd it start?" he asked.

"Bessie — was Bessie that done it," the barman replied in a hoarse voice.

Starbuck came around slowly to face Dison. Beyond, in the group that had gathered in the clearing, he could see Doc Gilman bending over someone.

"Doesn't make sense. Why would Bessie want to burn down her own place?"

Dison moved wearily. "Who knows? Went sort of crazy, I suspect. After you left, she come out of the room where McGraw's body'd been put — told us all to get out.

"Some of the boys had picked up Bart Fisher, was toting him out for burying. She hollered at them, made them put him on the bar, all the time yelling something about she was aiming to put an end to things right there. We figured it was best to humor her, so we done what she said.

"After we was out, she slammed the doors, and we heard her drop the pin lock to keep them shut. We set ourselves down then to wait, figuring she'd open up soon's she'd spent some time with Amos's body."

"Bessie the only one inside — except for McGraw and Fisher?"

Dison looked down. "Nope — that the worst part of it. We learned pretty quick she'd locked the women in their rooms — all but six or seven that happened to be downstairs and got drove out when she shut the doors."

Shawn felt his blood chill. "You mean they —"

"Burned up — right along with Bessie and McGraw and Fisher. It was pure hell, hearing them screaming and crying in there . . . Bessie must've poured coal oil from the lamps all through the place before she touched it off. There was a pretty fair wind blowing at the time, too, and they just wasn't a thing we could do. The whole place, from one end to the other, went up in no time."

A tremor passed through Starbuck. It was not difficult to imagine the holocaust — the roaring flames leaping through the dry wood, the cries of the trapped women so deeply hated by Bessie because of their youth and beauty and the supplanting part they had played in her life with Amos McGraw.

"I see you got your man," Pete said, "not that it matters much now . . . Who's them other two?"

Shawn brought himself back to the moment. "Hake Dallman and one of his bunch. They jumped us. We had to shoot it out with them."

Pete nodded. "Then you didn't —"

"No, it was one of them that killed him. He stood by me — again." Starbuck motioned toward the clearing. "What about them? Can't stay here."

"Don't aim to. Soon's everybody's able to travel — Doc's having to fix some of them up — we're headed for Dodge. We got plenty of horses, and we was able to save a couple of wagons and Amos's buggy."

"Did Jenny make it all right?"

"Yeh — Doc got her out of the hotel in time."

"Glad to hear that . . . I see my sorrel standing over there. I'll swap this buckskin for him after I'm through with the burying."

Dison nodded soberly. "Be pleased to help you. Reckon a fellow could say the graveyard's the only thing in Babylon that didn't go up in smoke . . . You riding on to Dodge with us?"

Starbuck looked off across the sea of buffalo grass. It stretched clean and fresh to the far horizon, undisturbed by the contingencies that alter the lives of men.

"No reason to. I'll head on to Santa Fe. Maybe I'll find out something about my brother there."